To the Edge of the World
MICHELE TORREY

LAUREL-LEAF BOOKS

Published by
Dell Laurel-Leaf
an imprint of
Random House Children's Books
a division of Random House, Inc.
New York

Visit us on the Web! www.randomhouse.com/teens

Educators and librarians, for a variety of teaching tools, visit us at
www.randomhouse.com/teachers

ISBN: 0-440-23793-9

RL: 6.2

Reprinted by arrangement with Alfred A. Knopf

Printed in the United States of America

First Dell Laurel-Leaf Edition December 2004

10 9 8 7 6 5 4 3 2 1

OPM

To Carl,
my love, my dearest love, always.

And to our sons,
Ian, Aaron, and Ethan.
May your lives be filled with adventure;
may you know the joys of courage,
of honor, and of love.

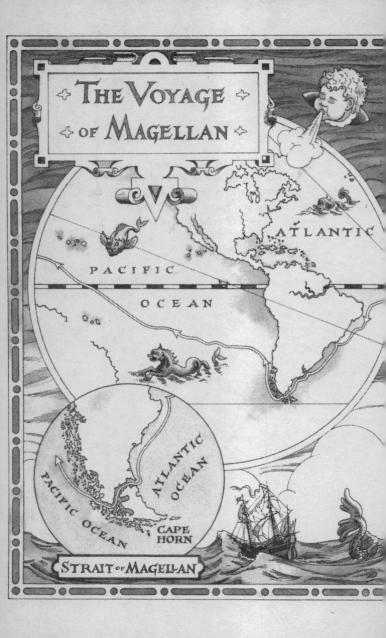

THE VOYAGE OF MAGELLAN

ATLANTIC

PACIFIC

OCEAN

PACIFIC OCEAN

ATLANTIC OCEAN

CAPE HORN

STRAIT of MAGELLAN

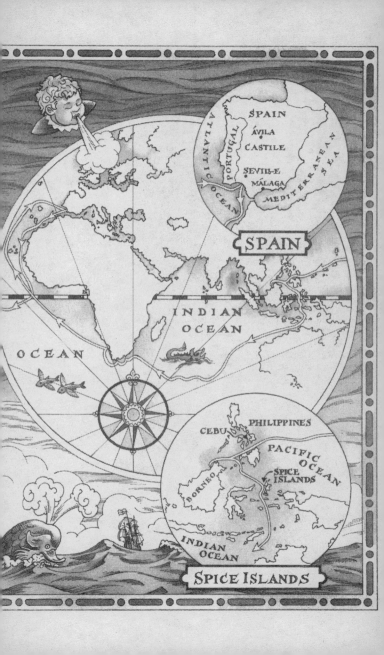

I
June 1519–July 1519

On the first day of June, in the year of our Lord 1519, I, Mateo Macías de Ávila, a Spaniard by birth, buried my parents.

An ugly dog watched. Spotted with mange, the dog lounged in the shadow of a nearby boulder, panting, his tongue lolling out of his mouth while I piled stone after stone upon their bodies. It did not take long before the sweat glistened on my body. The sun was fierce and no breeze blew. But I did not stop. I could not stop. I refused to stop, and my chest burned from the exertion.

I was determined. More determined than he. No dog would devour my parents. No dog would drag them through the city gates of Ávila like they dragged Juan Garcia, or young Catalina, to gnaw their flesh while the townspeople fled in horror. I threw a rock, but the dog dodged it deftly, ears flattened, returning quickly to his spot in the shade.

For much of the morning I worked, until finally I fell to my knees before the finished graves. "Father, Mother," I prayed. "Rest in peace." I reached out and touched the wooden crosses, caressed the names etched beneath my fingertips. I crossed myself and asked God to be merciful to their souls.

Afterward, I burned the farm.

My home. Dry, parched land, strewn with rock. A dusty courtyard, surrounded by a fence of sticks. A house of mud and stone. One room. A table. A chair. One rug. Two beds. A curtain dividing.

In spite of the heat, my eyes misted as I remembered. There beside the table, beside the planked surface where beeswax candles once burned, was where my mother read me poetry. To the pride of my father, she could read. "You will teach our son," Tomás had commanded, drawing himself up to his full height, despite his bad leg. "My son is not a peasant. My son will be someone. Read, María, read." My mother bent her head over her book, her only book, her voice soft as the flutter of birds' wings. After, she always said, "Mateo, my son, sing me a song." And I gladly fetched my guitar and sang while her eyes closed and my father tapped his good foot.

Now the table wavered with heat, and orange flames snapped and curled, devouring the curtain, the beds, the roof above my head. Smoke filled my nostrils and I stumbled backward out the door. I lay on my back in the courtyard, ashamed of my crying, not caring that the dog now lay panting beside me.

I lay like that until the fire drove me away. My possessions sat in a pile by the fence. I slung my guitar over my back and slipped my dagger into my waistband. I draped my mother's rosary about my neck and picked up the book of poems, my sketchbook of drawings and box of inks (for my mother had also taught me to draw), and a goatskin filled with watered wine. Into my shirt pocket I dropped two pieces of bread, hoping they would not fall through the frayed hole. My father refused to allow my mother to sew patches on our clothing. "Only the poor do such things," he said. And he was right. We were not poor.

I whacked the ugly dog on the nose with a stick, sending him howling, and tossed the stick into the fire. I watched until the only home I had known was but a blackened, crumbling shell.

By now the sun burned high in the sky. It was time to leave.

It took a long time to gather my father's sheep, frightened away by the dog and the fire. There were ten sheep, but I found only eight. I feared to stay longer lest the dreaded pestilence that consumed Ávila—devouring neighbors, friends, parents—also consume me.

And so, with eight sheep and my few possessions, I turned my back on the town of Ávila, turned my back on the two mounds of stone beside the smoking ruin. I set my face to the south and began to walk.

On the afternoon of the next day, I realized I was being followed. Perhaps he smelled the one last piece of bread that had not been eaten. Perhaps he thought he could steal one of my father's sheep. Or perhaps, and this at least I hoped was true, he despaired of digging at the graves of my parents. In any event, the ugly dog trotted behind me. Never close. But near enough so he shimmered in the heat, a speck of grime no bigger than a flea.

I ate my last piece of bread and drank the last of my wine. Then I checked my armpits for pestilence, then the sides of my neck and my groin. Nothing. I said the rosary.

The next day I turned fourteen years old. I lay in a ditch by a river, too hot, too weak to move. Never had I been so far from home. Never had I been so hungry.

When I awoke the next morning, the sheep were gone. Footprints marred the mud next to the river, and they were not mine. I looked everywhere and found only Ugly, lapping water at the river's edge. Anger grew within me like water coming to boil and I hurled a rock at him. "You could have warned me!" I cried, tears of frustration rising in my eyes. "Next time I will stab you with my dagger!"

When Ugly disappeared in the distance, I lay in the ditch and waited for the pestilence to take me to my parents. Without my father's sheep, I had nothing—nothing to sell, nothing to trade. I waited a long time to die. When the sun began to slide down in the sky, my stomach hurt worse than it had for days. Perhaps that was the first symptom. Again, I checked my armpits, my neck, my groin. Nothing. I did not say the rosary.

In the morning, when I knew I was not dead, I dragged myself out of the ditch and continued to journey southward.

At noon, I approached a monastery, nestled beneath the wing of a castle like a chick under a hen. From behind the monastery doors wafted a delicious aroma that made my stomach cramp with pain. I could stand it no more. To the ringing of the bell, I cast my glance to the ground and gathered in shame with others—ragged beggars, crippled children, one-legged soldiers—around a huge cauldron of soup. When my turn came, I dared to look into the face of the monk who handed me a bowl. Instead of the scowl I expected, I was met with a kindly look.

"May God bless you," he murmured as he ladled the steaming broth into my bowl. Into my other hand he thrust a hunk of bread. I sat upon a rock, devouring my food, not caring that the soup burned all the way down. Only when I finished and sat licking my fingers of every drop, every spare crumb, did I realize Ugly watched me. Under his accusing stare, the soup suddenly turned sour, and I vomited.

I was angry with myself and wondered blankly if I should eat the vomit, but when Ugly began to devour it, I returned to the monastery. The entrance was closed and I banged on the doors. The same monk who had served me my soup and bread answered, and there was a glint of recognition in his eye.

"I have vomited my soup and bread."

He disappeared and returned to give me another hunk of bread. But when I asked for more soup, my mouth watering and my belly aching to think of it, he said, "I'm sorry, but there is no more. We have given it all away. Come back tomorrow at noon."

I did not argue, and when the door closed softly, I steeled my face and turned away. I will not wait until the morrow, I told myself. I will not allow him to serve me again. I shall move on to the next town.

On the morrow I sat outside another monastery with bread and a bowl of soup in my hands. I forced myself to eat slowly.

Ugly licked his lips and watched me with eyes I noticed were brown. Sad and brown. I let Ugly have a bite of bread and, after I finished the broth, set the bowl down and watched while Ugly licked it out. This time I did not vomit.

The next day, when instead of a monastery there stretched a vast, empty plateau, Ugly caught a rabbit and left it at my feet. A bloody, furry mess that we ate together.

And so we passed out of the plateau, out of the land of Castile, into the lower countries of which I had only heard tell. Many rivers we crossed. Shallow, starved rivers that dreamed of rain. Each time I fell beside the muddy water, drinking until my stomach tightened like a goatskin. Beside me, after drinking his fill, Ugly lay on his back, exposing his spotted belly to the heavens, a belly full and bloated like my own.

In one of these rivers I lost my dagger. I waded into the river with all my possessions, but upon gaining the other side, I found that my dagger was gone. After searching for the better part of a day I admitted it was lost. I sat upon the muddy bank and cursed my life. What is a man without his dagger?

The next morning, I entered a side pool and sat in its still waters. I checked my reflection for signs of pestilence, but no disease stared back at me. Instead I saw the image of a young man, swarthy like his father, stocky, with a mop of unruly hair and an undignified nose. After staring at myself, I decided I was not nearly so ugly as Ugly, and the thought made me smile, startling me when straight white teeth smiled back.

After feasting on another rabbit, we waded across the river, the dog and I, and many rivers after, until we came to a land that slowly turned green, a land that smelled faintly of orange blossoms, of food, of the sea.

II

August 2, 1519

The inn reeked of smoke. Thick and acrid, it belched from the corner chimney, blackening the long central table, the benches, the walls, even the face of the woman who asked me what I wanted.

"A bed for the night," I replied.

"One real." She thrust out a grimy hand for the coin. When she saw my hesitation, her eyes narrowed. "No beggars. Get out." She turned and left me standing while the customers of the inn stared.

My face burned. Though I knew he was dead, it was as if my father watched me yet, his mouth set in a grim line, angry and ashamed. "I am not a beggar," I called after her. She appeared not to have heard me, instead bending over the fire and stirring it with a poker. "I will play my guitar. I will sing. Perhaps someone will give me money." She said nothing and I continued, trying to keep my voice low. "If I do not earn enough for a bed, I will leave."

She stood from the fire and faced me, her cheeks blackened with a fresh layer of soot. "Very well, but I pray you can carry a tune better than the last fellow. He bellowed like a sow in labor, and my husband had to throw him into the street in two pieces. It was very messy. Now get out from under my feet and leave me alone. I have work to do."

I mumbled my thanks and sat in the corner farthest from the fire. It was evening, and more men piled through the greasy doorway to sit at the one table stretching through the center of the room. Wine flowed freely.

I tuned my guitar to gales of spluttering, half-drunken laughter. Praying for mercy from the Blessed Virgin, I began to sing. I sang of El Cid—of his battles, his adventures, his heroism. It was a beautiful ballad and one of my father's favorites. When I finished, my voice trailed into silence. The laughter continued.

I sang again. I sang until my voice clogged with smoke and my tongue stumbled. I sang until men drooped under the table, drunk with wine, their spaces on the bench quickly filled by others, others who laughed and sang their own songs. I sang until the food smells made my stomach clench with hunger. No one had yet given me a coin. Again I would be forced to sleep on the streets of Málaga with Ugly. Then as my voice cracked and my fingers turned numb, I noticed what I should have noticed before.

A man. Watching me.

He was perhaps twice my age, maybe more. His face was strong, sun-browned, and chiseled like a soldier's. "Are you hungry?" he asked after I finished singing.

I slung my guitar over my back and prepared to leave. "No."

"Come. Sit with me. I have brought too much food and need someone to share it with."

I looked to see if he mocked me, but he only smiled. I

shrugged, propped the guitar against the wall, and sat next to him on the bench.

He motioned to the woman. "Wine and a pallet for the boy. And cook this with onion and garlic." Out of a saddlebag he pulled a rabbit, freshly dead by the look of it.

The woman grabbed the rabbit by the ears, held out her hand for the onions and garlic, and then stormed away.

I tried not to lick my lips when he withdrew bread and cheese, a handful of figs, and two oranges, so fragrant I smelled them despite the smoke. He set them on the splintered table and, without saying a word, tore off a chunk of bread and shoved the rest of the round loaf at me. He did the same with the cheese.

I stuffed bread and cheese in my mouth while I peeled an orange. A cup of wine appeared as if by magic before me, and I drank deeply, not caring that it stank of hide and pitch and tasted of goatskin.

As I chewed a mouthful of figs, I realized the man was talking to me, but hunger had clogged my ears.

"You are from Málaga?"

"Ávila."

"Ávila! That is in the heart of Castile. My friend, you are far from home."

"I have traveled for two months."

"You walked?"

"Walked, rode on the backs of carts." I lowered my voice. "Once I stole a donkey and rode him, but an hour out of the village, the donkey dropped dead. He must have been sick."

"Very unlucky, my friend. Even so, to walk such a distance at a time when even the stones are made to melt is a true measure of any man. What is your name?"

I swallowed my figs and puffed out my chest. "Mateo Macías de Ávila."

"Well met, Mateo. And I am Gonzalo Gómez de Espinosa, born in the Cantabrian Mountains of Old Castile. You may call me Espinosa."

Old Castile? Indeed, he had the blue eyes of a Basque, eyes like my mother's, and he appeared strong, broad-shouldered, as rugged as my father. But there was something else about him that intrigued me more—the way he carried himself.

I remembered one day when I was very young, I stood outside the walls of Ávila and gaped while mounted soldiers, each wearing a scallop shell around his neck, rode through the city gates and disappeared into the heat beyond. "They are the Knights of the Order of Santiago," my father said. "They have defended our castles against the Moors. They ransomed Christian captives and liberated those of the true faith from the infidels." And although I did not understand, I remembered the way the knights sat in the saddles— their pride, their discipline. Espinosa reminded me of these men.

"Tell me, my young Mateo, do you steal often?"

Espinosa's casual words caused the chunk of bread to stick in my throat. I tried to swallow but could not. A dozen thoughts plowed through my mind in an instant. Why does he ask you such a thing? *Because he is the donkey man! He asks you this because it was his donkey you stole!* He has followed you from Castile, following your tracks in the muddy rivers. He will stick you in the ribs and never believe you when you say it was the only thing you have ever stolen. He will not care that your mother's voice clanged in your ears for days afterward, ringing over and over *Thou shalt not steal! Thou shalt not steal!* until you clamped your hands over your ears and screamed for mercy!

Now I looked about me for a way to escape. A way to defend myself. Anchored by a chain in the middle of the table was a communal knife.

I lunged for the knife.

Espinosa's hand crushed my wrist in a grip so strong it made me gasp with pain. I had not even seen him move.

"Put it down," he said calmly.

I did so. I sat upon the bench and rubbed my wrist, feeling the gaze of everyone upon me. Each stare burned like a hot poker in my flesh. *Thief! Thief!* For the second time that evening, my face burned with shame.

Then to my surprise, Espinosa smiled. It was not a ruthless smile—the smile of a killer before he rips out your liver—it was instead a smile of friendship. "Forgive me, young Mateo. I did not mean to injure your fierce Castilian pride."

A few around the table chuckled. Did they mock me? "Be careful," one of them warned, a man with a cleft lip and a pate so bald it reflected the candlelight. "He seeks to recruit you for an ocean voyage."

Another man with blackened teeth nodded. "Take my advice, boy, don't go. They pay only enough to buy a few mouse turds at the end of it, that is if you make it back at all. You'd be better off to embark on a short voyage, a voyage whose destination is no secret. At least you'll come back alive."

The room resounded with grunts of agreement.

"Tell me," said Espinosa, "how old are you?"

I opened my mouth to say seventeen, but instead the truth came out. "Fourteen."

"Where are your parents?"

I opened my mouth to say I had no parents but told the truth once more. "They died of pestilence," I said softly. Immediately upon my words, the room exploded with cursing, and all except Espinosa either left the inn or rushed to sit at the opposite end of the table.

Now we were quite alone.

The woman returned with a pot of rabbit stew, bubbling and fragrant.

As if loathe to come too close, she flung the pot on the table, along with bowls and utensils. We jumped back as stew slopped onto the planks. "Serve yourselves," she snapped. "That's six reals you owe me. I should charge you double, triple even. Thanks to you, I've lost my best customers."

Espinosa tossed the coins at her, and she scooped them off the dirt floor, muttering curses under her breath.

The stew tasted delicious. I closed my eyes to savor its goodness. Food, I thought. I finally have food. Real food. Food like my mother used to prepare. For a moment I pretended I was home and that her voice danced as she read me poems.

Instead of my mother's voice, I heard Espinosa's. "I am sorry," he said.

"Sorry?" I opened my eyes.

"About your parents."

A sudden lump formed in my throat, and I blinked back tears. That he should see me like this made me ashamed. My father never cried. Never. And I could not stop the grief inside my chest, bubbling like rabbit stew, hot and scalding.

"Have you no other relatives?"

I shook my head and tears fell like rain.

"Your father's family?"

"They are dead, too."

"Your mother's family?"

"I do not know who they are." I hesitated. "There is no one."

With a square, scar-ridden hand he reached out and patted my shoulder. For a long while he said nothing and I began to eat again.

"You are hungry, and yet you grieve. It is a hard combination for any man. I am sorry life has dealt you such a cruel blow, Mateo. But perhaps I can help you. I do seek men for a voyage. Strong, courageous men like you, built hard and tough, able to raise sail if need be or row a boat through rough waters. It matters not that you have no experience, for I need you also for your music. For your guitar."

I wiped my nose on my sleeve and looked at him.

"That will be your job. Cabin boy, yes, but also musician. During such a long voyage, the men need music."

"How long a voyage?"

"Some recruiters tell the men four months. But, like you, I will be honest." Espinosa took a deep drink of his wine, paused, and looked straight at me. "I require two years of your life, Mateo Macías de Ávila. Two years that I cannot say will be easy, for we go to a destination unknown. You will have no luxuries. No special privileges. But you will have food, companionship, and work, and that is more than you have now. Perhaps you will forget your sorrow. I leave in the morning for Seville, and by then you must decide."

III
August 10, 1519

The heat rose in waves and sweat trickled down my chest and under my arms. The stench of sewage hung in the air. Five ships, their hulls freshly blackened with tar, creaked and swayed.

Beside me, Ugly stretched and yawned, then sat on his haunches and looked at me, panting. I stood on the docks of Seville in a crush of men. I had been told there were Africans, Portuguese, Sicilians, French, Germans, Greeks, Flemings, English, Genoese, and Spanish—a crew more than two hundred and seventy strong.

All of us faced an altar, and upon its surface burned many candles. Black smoke disappeared into the cloudless sky. Wax melted and puddled. Before us stood the archbishop of Seville, dressed in his colorful vestments, waiting as we waited. It was the day decreed by King Carlos for the departure of the armada. The captains of the voyage had yet to arrive.

For a long time the only movements were the seabirds as they swooped overhead or strutted among our legs, screeching whenever Ugly growled.

Then, in the distance, I heard thunder. The thunder grew until it became the roar of many hooves pounding the streets.

"They come," the man beside me whispered.

I made the sign of the cross.

Now they appeared. The glint of armor, of lances. The colorful banners whipping on the ends of long poles. The people of the streets pressed against the buildings to allow them passage. The darkened, foaming flanks of horses. Hard faces under helmets of steel.

In a hollow clatter of hooves, they wheeled to a stop on the docks. Dismounting, they handed the reins to servants who led the horses away. Each in full armor, the captains knelt before the altar. Those who had ridden with them now held the banners aloft, and upon each banner waved a coat of arms.

I recognized Espinosa, suited in dazzling armor that reflected the light of the sun. While at the inn, he had told me his position aboard the fleet. He was master-at-arms. It was he who was in charge of all the marines; it was he who would lead any attacks ordered by the commander. Today, lines of marines stood at attention behind him, and my chest swelled with pride. I knew this man.

"In nomine Patris," intoned the archbishop, making the sign of the cross, *"et Filii, et Spiritus Sancti."*

With those words, the Mass began.

I glanced at the man next to me. He was, perhaps, only a couple of years older than I, trim and lean, with brown hair and a nose curved like a blade. As if feeling my gaze upon him, he hacked and spat and glanced at me, his eyes in a squint, penetrating and mean. But when he spoke, he sounded ordinary enough. "To what ship are you assigned?" he asked.

15

"The *San Antonio*."

He grunted and spat again. "Likewise."

Together we watched the Mass, murmuring our responses, kneeling when required.

"Your position?" he asked.

"Cabin boy and musician. Yours?"

"Servant to Captain Cartagena of Castile."

We talked in hushed voices while the archbishop gave his sermon. The servant's name was Rodrigo Nieto, and like me, he hailed from Castile. He had run away from home for an adventurous life at sea.

"Have you been to sea before?" I asked him.

"Just returned a week ago."

"Someone told me yesterday that I am an idiot for going to sea. That I would have been better to stay home, pestilence or not." I leaned toward him. "Is it true what he said, that every hour is spent swabbing decks? That it is backbreaking and boring? Is it true that it is not as adventurous as is told?"

Rodrigo regarded me. "Do you see all these men before you?"

I nodded.

"If we are lucky, half of us will return. It is the way of the sea. And that, my friend, is what I call adventure."

A silver bell jangled. I turned from Rodrigo and focused on the wafer that the archbishop held high. *"Hoc est enim corpus meum. . . ."*

Rodrigo's words rang in my head like the silver bell of Communion. Is this true? I wondered. Did I stand only half a chance of setting my feet once more upon the soil of Spain?

Again Rodrigo spoke, "It is whispered we sail to the Spice

Islands through waters never before seen by civilized man. Dangerous waters where cannibals roast a sailor's skin while he is yet alive, where two-headed monsters spit flame from their mouths and backsides." In answer to my look of disbelief he added, "Why do you think so few Spaniards have signed for this voyage? And why do you think there are so many stupid foreigners?" He spat again, and his voice hardened. "Even the captain-general, the captain of all captains, is Portuguese."

"Portuguese? How can that be? This is a Spanish expedition!"

"Hush. Keep your voice low. We do not want to draw attention." Rodrigo paused as we both went forward and took Communion. Returning to our places, he continued quietly, "It is true. The captain-general is Portuguese. See? He is over there. Fernando de Magallanes is his name. Nothing but a petty nobleman."

I watched as the man Rodrigo pointed to knelt before the altar and swore an oath of allegiance to King Carlos of Spain. The captain-general was suited in armor, and from a distance away, it was difficult for me to see what he looked like. I knew only that he was swarthy and seemed old—forty, perhaps. A Portuguese to lead the Spanish armada? A petty nobleman, only? And old, besides?

Rodrigo was whispering, "I tell you I would not have signed for the voyage were it not for the riches promised at the end."

"Riches?"

"Aye. Enough spices—cloves, nutmeg, pepper—to fill every pocket of every man, each grain worth more than life itself. Not only that, it is said there will be so much gold and rubies, diamonds and emeralds, that those of us who return will bathe in them each day as if they were water. That we will live in castles with many servants and eat spicy foods and never have to work again."

My jaw dropped and I stared at Rodrigo. I tried to imagine such riches, gold and jewels, but could not. In my mind I saw only my mother's faded dresses, trimmed with yellowed lace and stitched with dirty, knotted, golden threads. My tongue could not imagine spices either, for I had never tasted such things. Spices were for kings and princes. Even so, I thought, Today I am lucky. I leave on a voyage and shall return a wealthy man. I will bathe in diamonds, eat spices, and never work again.

Rodrigo caught me staring. "Remember, my friend, we must battle two-headed monsters and escape from cannibals before we live like kings in castles. It is said cannibals love the taste of the human tongue. And if you think you will just chop out your tongue and give it to them, sailing away mute but rich, let me tell you what else they love. . . ."

As Rodrigo filled my ears with a list of body parts, I turned back toward the altar. Magallanes stood proudly and received the silken royal standard. Steel clashed against steel as the four other captains and the officers of the fleet knelt before him. In one voice they swore obedience to him, their captain-general. To follow none but him. To Magallanes they gave the power of life and death. Power "of the knife and the rope."

". . . and finally," whispered Rodrigo, "they will grind your bones to powder and drink the powder mixed with your blood. Bone soup, they call it. It is their favorite. A delicacy."

"*Ite, Missa est,*" said the archbishop, dismissing us.

"*Deo gratias,*" I replied, shivering as if someone already drank my bones.

* * *

I was issued a sea chest and a roll of bedding, the cost of which would be taken from my pay. Into the sea chest I placed my belongings—my sketchbook and inks, my book of poems, my goatskin, my rosary—all I owned except my guitar, as it was too big.

My sea chest looked empty, but Rodrigo said to take heart. Soon it would fill with rubies and diamonds, pearls and emeralds, gold and silk. Already Rodrigo was hurrying up the gangplank of the *San Antonio,* urging me to follow. "Hurry. Before all the good spots are taken."

I paused and knelt beside Ugly. "And you, my friend, shall have a new rib bone each day to chew. You will fatten with fresh meat, and we will never be hungry again."

As if he understood, Ugly licked his lips and thumped his tail upon the dock.

"Come, boy," I said, slinging my guitar across my back. "Before they leave without us." Giddy with adventure, I followed Rodrigo up the gangplank. Ugly trotted behind me.

"Are you crazy?" Rodrigo hissed once I stepped aboard. "You can't bring the dog! Get rid of him now before we're both in trouble."

I set down my things, blinking with surprise. "Who says I can't bring him?"

"How should I know? Only that you can't. No one has before."

"Then I shall be the first," I said, thumping my chest. "Besides, I cannot leave him behind. He's my friend. He follows me everywhere."

"That mangy thing? Your friend?" Rodrigo burst into laughter and slapped his knee.

I shifted my feet. Men from all over the ship now stared at me—and at Ugly. My ears burned with embarrassment. "Stop laughing, Rodrigo. Everyone stares."

But it was too late. A marine approached us, and I could tell by the set of his jaw and the churning in my stomach that I was already in trouble.

"No dogs." His voice was clipped and heavy with importance, his face pockmarked like a rutted road.

I faced the marine, drawing myself up to my tallest. Even so, the top of my head came no higher than his chin. "You do not understand," I replied. "My dog is special. He is a very good hunter, and he—"

"No dogs."

"—but—but he won't be any trouble. He does everything I tell him, and he's very smart—"

The marine drew his sword, lowered his face into mine, and barked, "Take him off the ship now or I will skewer him like a pig!" Flecks of spit landed on my face.

I stood, speechless. The world seemed to have stopped. Every sailor, every captain, every man in Seville, everyone in all of Spain, for that matter, stared at me, breathless, to see what I would do.

Into that silence, Ugly bared his teeth, growling. His hackles raised.

For a brief moment in which every muscle of my body tensed, I considered giving Ugly the signal to attack. To sink his fangs into that pockmarked throat. It would be so easy, so satisfying. But, angry as I was, I knew Ugly would only die for it. If the marine did not slay him, someone else would. Instead I clenched my jaw, turned, and marched down the gangplank, followed by the patter of dog paws, hot tears pressing against my eyes.

I left him on the dock, lost in a swirl of people. "Stay," I told him. "Stay here. I have a different life now. Very different." Then I walked away without looking back.

IV

September 20–October 2, 1519

There was the constant swelling and swaying beneath my feet. I could not walk a straight line. My stomach churned. I heaved my dinner of sardines, biscuit, cheese, and raisins over the railing and into the sea, thinking, So this is it. My new life.

Rodrigo spat and called me a weakling. "This is nothing. Wait until we hit upon waters not so calm. Then you will retch your guts out and wish you were dead."

If that was not bad enough, Rodrigo and I quartered with the rest of the crew in the exposed waist deck in the center of the ship. It was noisy and crowded. There was no such thing as privacy. There were fifty, sixty of us, elbowing each other for room. Cabin boys, soldiers, seamen, coopers, barbers, gunners . . . "What will happen when it rains?" I asked anxiously, gazing into the sky.

Rodrigo snorted with impatience. "You will get wet, of course." Then he swaggered away, shaking his head, mumbling, "Landlubber."

Later, before the sun sank on this, my first day at sea, I drew one of the ships—the flagship *Trinidad*—in my sketchbook. From the time I was little, my mother had taught me to draw. It came easily to me. Whenever I drew, the world became lost, as if I were elsewhere. As if I still heard her voice saying, "Find your light source, Mateo. See it in your mind. Is it the sun? The moon? A candle? Now see the shadows. Light and dark, my son, they belong together."

With quick, easy strokes, I sketched the *Trinidad*'s deep-bellied hull, her colorful decorations bow and stern, her three masts, her multitude of square and triangular sails, the jumble of rigging. I drew the royal standard of Castile flying atop the mainmast and the banner of the Holy Trinity flying from the foremast. In the waist of the ship I sketched the banner of the captain-general, Magallanes.

The next day, I awoke to a seabird screeching in my ear. Ears ringing, I cuffed the empty air with my fist, cursing as the bird flew to the yard. "You'd better get up," warned Rodrigo. "I've been trying to wake you, but you sleep like the dead. It's eight bells and our watch has begun."

I stumbled to my feet, yawning, rubbing sleep from my eyes, anxious to prove I was no landlubber. "I am ready," I said, steeling my voice and my stomach.

And so, with Rodrigo's help, my duties began.

Because there was no cook aboard, the apprentice seaman on watch cooked for the crew. Rodrigo and I, however, cooked the food for the captain and the high-ranking officers of the *San Antonio*. I felt proud to have such an important job.

We lit a fire in a sandbox on the leeward side of the fo'c'sle— the side facing away from the wind. (*Leeward* . . . *fo'c'sle* . . . it was the language of sailors . . . and I was now a sailor.) The sandbox was protected on three sides by built-up walls. And although the sun shone as hot and fierce as in Castile, the ocean breeze cooled my bare back as I crouched over the open side of the sandbox, stirring stews as smoke wisped away from the ship.

During my watch, I played my guitar and sang while the men worked. When I was not singing or cooking the officers' meals, I swabbed decks and polished the metalworks, learning the chanteys the men sang. There was a rhythm to the work. I began to enjoy it. To look forward to each morning when, at eight bells and the change of watches, we started each day with prayers led by the padre.

One evening while we cooked, Rodrigo whispered that he, along with seven other servants, waited on Cartagena at the table in his cabin, dabbing his mouth with a napkin following each bite. They polished his armor again and again. Six times a day they laid out fresh clothes for Cartagena to wear, helping their captain out of the old clothes and into the new. "In his clothing trunk there are sights to behold, Mateo. Gold-threaded jackets, velvet hats, breeches of swan skin, shirts of Castilian silk, a material so fine you would swear it was the smooth flesh of a woman. I tell you, Mateo, when I am rich, I, too, shall have such finery."

I could scarce imagine such riches when all I had was my one shirt and pair of breeches.

On the fourth day at sea, the captain strolled from his cabin onto the sun-filled deck. I stopped polishing the metalworks to stare. Never in my life had I seen such a fine man. He was young—perhaps only five and twenty—and tall, standing with the stately bearing of one born into nobility. Like most Spanish nobles, he had fair hair and blue eyes. He sported a small, pointed mustache over full, sensuous lips. I knew the mustache was meticulously oiled and groomed after each meal, for Rodrigo had told me so.

At the captain's side stood two dogs. A twinge of resentment stole over me, but I squared my shoulders, determined not to spoil such a moment. Cartagena's dogs were black, square-jawed, and massive. A spiked iron collar circled each of their necks. The captain laid a long, tapering hand on their heads. They whined and their tails wagged and they smacked their lips with long tongues. "Carry on," said Cartagena with a wave of his hand, and it was only then that I realized that our chantey had faded into silence. The entire larboard watch had ceased their work and stared at Cartagena.

I continued to polish, occasionally glancing at the captain. So this was the man who would lead the *San Antonio*. This was the man on whom our lives depended. Indeed, he was a fine man, with fine dogs. I am Mateo Macías of the *San Antonio,* I said to myself, assigned to the largest, most magnificent vessel of the fleet, where a dignified Castilian rules as captain.

The next day the captain called us aft for a reading of the shipboard rules, written by King Carlos himself and commanded to be read aloud upon departure. As I listened, the breeze blew my hair from my face. The main sail snapped. The yard groaned. Still Cartagena read. Page after page. At first, his dogs sat beside him, gazing at him, wagging their tails, but after a while they lay down and fell asleep. There were rules for the conduct of officers—how to treat native chiefs, how to trade, precisely where to set up shore camps, and how to treat the sick. There were also rules for conduct of the common crew—no molesting of native women, no swearing, no playing cards, no dice.

25

". . . for from such often arises evil and scandal and strife." Cartagena stopped reading, as if the words had suddenly lodged in his throat like a rotted hunk of food. He frowned, skimmed the last ten pages or so, and finally added, "Ad infinitum, ad infinitum." Then, much to our relief, he dismissed us with a wave of his hand. As we walked away, Rodrigo grumbled that surely King Carlos was the Mother Mary in disguise, for no one but her could invent so many rules.

On the sixth day we arrived at the Canary Islands, a paradise of blue seas and white sands. The beaches swarmed with natives—handsome men, beautiful girls, their hair braided with flowers such as I'd never seen before. I went ashore and drew a tree in my sketchbook. The tree was stumpy, with a thick trunk that wept blood-colored sap. From the tops of gnarled branches grew clusters of sword-shaped leaves and orange berries. For a tree, it was impressive. But when Rodrigo saw my drawing, he laughed, asking why I did not draw a girl instead. I felt myself flush and told him to mind his own business. What did he know? My tree was very good.

One day while at the islands, a ship arrived. She moored at the docks, and from where I stood on the *San Antonio*, I saw the banners of Spain wave upon her halyards. What was a Spanish ship doing here? I wondered. Was she to join our fleet? Would we now have six ships?

I heard a muttered curse. Captain Cartagena was standing beside me, a full head taller than I. He paid me no attention, and I followed his gaze to see where he looked. In the waning light, a man disembarked the ship and trotted along the dock, illuminated first by one lantern, then another. Answering none of the questions darting at him from every side, he boarded the *Trinidad*, Magallanes's flagship, and entered the captain-general's cabin. As the door closed behind the man, Cartagena pounded his fist on the rail. "It is a message for Magallanes! This bodes not well."

I glanced around but saw no one. Had he spoken to me? "Excuse me, Captain?"

He looked at me as if he had not known I was there. And in that brief, unguarded instant, I saw hatred in his eyes. Even as I glimpsed this, the corner of his lips curved up into a smile and his eyes softened. Now they contained no hint of hatred. Had I imagined it?

"Forgive me," said Cartagena. "I did not know I spoke aloud."

I said nothing, at a loss for words before the great and handsome captain.

He continued to regard me. "Your name?"

I stood as tall as I could. "Mateo Macías de Ávila."

"Ah. A Castilian like myself. That is good. I have had quite enough of foreigners." He leaned against the rail and twisted the point of his delicate mustache between his thumb and finger. "Tell me, this messenger, what news do you think he brings from Spain?"

Captain Cartagena was asking me—*me*—my opinion. "Perhaps they are to join our fleet. Perhaps we will now have six ships rather than five."

"And I suppose you wish to be captain of this sixth ship?"

I reddened. "Of—of course not. I only—"

"Ah, do not be ashamed of ambition, boy. Ambition has crowned kings and emperors. Ambition, how shall I say, is capable of moving mountains when in the hands of the right man. Isn't that right, boy?"

27

"I suppose so."

"And I, I shall move mountains this voyage, else die trying." This he murmured to himself, gazing back toward the newly arrived ship. After a minute of silence, Cartagena turned again to me. "Tell me, what is it you have ambition for?"

"What do you mean?"

"What do you want from life, boy? Money? Power? Women? A man must know what he wants, else life becomes like water in his hands. It trickles away and still he thirsts. To know what you want, boy, that is ambition. Well?"

"I—I don't know."

"Do you want money?"

I thought of diamond baths. Castles. Servants. Never working again. "Yes."

"Power?"

"Of course. All wealthy men have great power."

"Women?"

I licked my lips, remembering Rodrigo's taunts, feeling my face redden again. "Of course. Many women. Who would not?"

"You see, boy, we think alike. Now tell me. What rumors have you heard?"

"Rumors? I—I don't understand."

"Everyone knows rumors fester on a ship like pox on a harlot, and a captain needs ears beyond what he himself can hear. A smart boy like yourself should catch hint of every rumor that flies by." He patted my shoulder. "Come, boy, don't be shy; tell me. Whatever it is, I promise, it is safe with me."

I answered in a gush of words. "They say that we travel to the Spice Islands through waters unknown to man. That if we are not

28

eaten by cannibals or sea monsters, it will be a quick, easy journey to a warm land of cloves, and we will return to Spain laden with chests of gold, rubies, pearls, and spices, and we will live like rich men in castles with many servants and much food and will never work again until we die."

At this, Cartagena threw back his head and laughed. He slapped me on the back. "You have lightened my mood, and indeed you have sharp eyes and ears, and a keen tongue. I can use a boy like you."

That night as I drifted to sleep, Cartagena's words echoed through my head. *I can use a boy like you. . . . I can use a boy like you.* I rolled over and fell into a warm, dreamless sleep.

A few days later, as night fell, I received a summons to the captain's cabin. Cartagena reclined in a cushioned chair, and while one servant buffed the nails of his left hand, another did the same on his right. A third servant shined the buckles on his shoes while a fourth polished the buttons on his jacket. Yet another held a plate of candied dates, which Cartagena refused. My mouth watered to see such treats, and my gaze followed the servant as he put the dates away.

Behind Cartagena I saw Rodrigo, stiff and formal, fill a goblet with wine and offer it to the captain.

Cartagena shook a servant from his hand, took the goblet, and sipped delicately, like a woman. He swallowed, saying, "Ah, Mateo, there you are. I have good news. The captains and pilots of all the ships are to meet this evening aboard the *Trinidad*. No doubt we will discover the contents of the message from Spain." He looked around him as if to notice the flurry of servants for the first time. "Leave us, all of you. Except the boy and Rodrigo."

Behind him, Rodrigo raised his eyebrows but said nothing as

the room emptied. "I trust the two of you can follow my orders? Yes? Very well then. During the meeting, you must hide where I tell you. Follow me and I shall show you what I mean. Hurry, we are late."

My heart racing, I jumped to do his bidding. We were going on a mission for Captain Cartagena! Together Rodrigo and I buttoned his blouse and draped his cloak about him. Before we left, Cartagena slipped a dagger into his waistband. "For protection," he said, drawing his cloak about him.

Once on the docks, Cartagena showed us where to hide. I looked around and realized why this was important. Concealed by darkness and atop casks of cargo, we could easily see through the *Trinidad*'s window hatches into Magallanes's lighted cabin. Once atop the casks, we edged closer. If I leaned forward over the water, I could almost touch the openings.

"Stay here until I fetch you." In a few moments we saw Cartagena enter Magallanes's cabin. Apparently, he was the last to arrive, for once he entered, the meeting was called to order.

We heard nothing of what they said.

A cold sweat came over me. I suddenly realized what we were doing. We perched atop casks of cargo, a cabin boy and a servant, spying on a meeting between captains and pilots. Why had Cartagena ordered us to spy? What would happen if we were caught? Too late I wished I hadn't agreed to go on the mission, but now I had no choice. And a cabin boy does not refuse to obey his captain. I glanced around nervously, but the darkness shrouded us like Cartagena's cloak, the water black as ink, and I saw nothing beyond the casks.

I turned back toward the light and peered into the room. The only time I had seen the other captains and pilots, they had been suited in full armor. Now, studying their faces, I recognized the captain-general. He was short and swarthy, a typical Portuguese with a black bushy beard, dark brooding eyes, and legs bowed like a peasant.

Beside me, Rodrigo whispered, his voice so soft I scarce heard him amid the creaking of the ship's timbers and the soft slap of water against the hull. "Magallanes looks like a sorry rat compared to our fine captain."

Magallanes circled the table, a table heaped with maps and charts, around which the captains and pilots were seated. The captain-general had a pronounced limp and suddenly reminded me of my father, the memory so sharp that for a moment I almost called his name. Idiot! I told myself. This dark, limping foreigner is not your father! Your father was Castilian, not Portuguese! Your father was a good man, a brave man, a righteous man! Yet my heart felt drained.

Magallanes stopped circling the table and sank into a chair. He looked tired, defeated. The captains and pilots around the table stared stonily at the captain-general. It looked to me as if they all hated Magallanes.

Now Cartagena commanded everyone's attention. He strutted about the table in a manner worthy of a Castilian, glancing with scorn at the captain-general. Finally, Cartagena stopped in front of Magallanes and leaned over him. He sneered and spat words at the little man. Magallanes raised his hands helplessly.

Rodrigo snarled through clenched teeth, "If Magallanes was truly a man, he would run Cartagena through with his sword. As anyone can see, Magallanes is a coward. He has no pride. No

31

honor. It is well Cartagena has brought his dagger. He will skewer Magallanes like a pig, and then we will have a true man to lead the armada."

I narrowed my eyes at Magallanes, for I agreed with Rodrigo. Such a weak, sniveling man, I thought. He is nothing like my father.

I continued to watch. Although Cartagena's hand moved toward his dagger many times, he did not draw it, for with each weak gesture from Magallanes, Cartagena seemed unsure. It was as if he wished for Magallanes to give him a reason to stab him. Cartagena's gaze flicked to others around the table as though asking what he should do.

It was then the casks beneath us began to shift and rock. While I yet wondered what it was, a hand wrapped itself around my ankle.

"Spies! I've found spies!"

V

October 2-25, 1519

Horror spread through my body with a sickening wave as both Rodrigo and I were yanked by our ankles from the casks.

I found myself gasping, lying flat on my stomach upon the dock, but before I could gather my wits, someone hauled me to my feet and dragged me by my ear toward the *Trinidad.* I had no choice but to follow.

From the light of the lanterns, I glimpsed Rodrigo's face and knew him to be as terrified as I. The man who held our ears was the marine with the pockmarked face. His eyes glittered in the lamplight.

"Idiot boys," he hissed under his breath.

The marine thrust us into Magallanes's cabin. The door closed. Light from candle flames flickered off the faces of captains and pilots. Faces that stared at me. The cabin reeked of candle smoke. Of dinner. Of sweat. Even of fear. A heavy silence pressed upon me, hot as my shame.

The captain-general, who had sat in his chair regarding us with a brooding, unreadable expression, now sighed and rose to his feet. His shoulders drooped and he scowled, his dark brows drawing together. "Spies?" he asked.

Desperate, I looked to Cartagena. My heart swelled with horror when he regarded me coolly, as if he had never seen me before, as if he knew not my name.

Magallanes faced me, and suddenly he did not seem the weak, sniveling creature I had observed through the window hatch. And although my knees quaked, I thrust up my chin. "I am not a spy," I said, surprised my voice sounded so calm.

"Perhaps," he replied softly, "you are a spy and a liar as well."

I made no answer, fearing what he might say next.

His gaze darted from me to Rodrigo.

Rodrigo stared unblinking into the captain-general's eyes. And when Magallanes began to turn away, Rodrigo spat, the spittle landing on Magallanes's boot.

An unearthly silence filled the room.

Magallanes stared at his boot, blinking, making no move to wipe the spit away.

Then for the first time since our entrance, Cartagena spoke. "Kill them."

I was grabbed and my arms thrust behind me. The marine bound my wrists with strong cord. I should have spoken aloud. I should have told them that Cartagena had commanded us to spy, but my mouth filled with dryness and I could not speak. My pride was too great. And in that moment, I hated Cartagena.

The marine pulled us toward the door.

"Wait," said Magallanes, with a wave of his hand. He turned to gaze at me. "These boys. To which ship are they assigned?"

"The *San Antonio*," someone replied.

Magallanes closed his eyes and sighed. We waited while he said nothing, his forehead creased with thought. Finally, he spoke, "My cabin boy jumped ship yesterday." He paused before continuing. "Reassign these crewmen to the *Trinidad*. Captain Cartagena should no longer be burdened with such scum. Their conduct shall now be my responsibility."

I glanced at Cartagena. A look of triumph spread over the young captain's face, a look which he quickly masked. His lips curled slightly. "As you wish, Captain-General." In a swirl of Castilian wool, he gathered his cloak about him, bowed to Magallanes, and left.

Rodrigo and I returned to the *San Antonio* for our possessions.

"Why didn't Cartagena tell him we were only following orders?" I asked angrily, kicking my bedding.

Rodrigo smiled. "Did you see the way I handled the captain-general?"

I slammed my sea chest closed and cinched the straps tight. "And why did Cartagena order us killed? What would have happened if Magallanes had agreed? What then?"

Rodrigo folded a shirt and placed it in his sea chest. "I would spit on his boot again if I had the chance. A hundred times. A thousand. Portuguese pig."

"Rodrigo! You're not listening to me!"

"Why should I? You're boring and have only one thing to say. Besides, you have not said anything about how I humiliated the captain-general."

"What do you want me to say? That you are a fine spitter and have great accuracy?"

"All right," answered Rodrigo.

"All right, what?"

"All right, you may say that."

"For the sake of God, Rodrigo, this is serious!"

Just then, a dog growled, low and deep-chested. I turned, startled. Cartagena stood stooped under the shadow of the quarterdeck. Now he stepped into the lantern light of the waist deck, along with his two massive dogs. "Congratulations. You managed to fool a crusty old commander. You played your parts to perfection, as I had hoped. My compliments to both of you for a job well done." Cartagena made a sweeping bow as a mocking smile played at the corner of his lips.

I narrowed my eyes. "We could have been killed! Why did you—"

"Mateo!" hissed Rodrigo, a look of caution blazing in his eyes.

One of the dogs growled. Cartagena laid a hand upon its head, sighing heavily. "Listen carefully, both of you, I've not much time. You must find that message from Spain. When I questioned Magallanes about it, he said it was of a personal family nature, but he is a liar. You must find it and report to me all you see and hear."

So that was it! He had planned the whole thing so we could become his spies aboard the *Trinidad*! "I will not spy for you," I said. "You used us."

With a look of irritation, he waved his hand to silence me. "No harm would have come to you, I assure you. Come, boy, what do you think of me? Do you think me a murderer?"

I crossed my arms.

"Believe me, boy, it was a calculated risk. I knew Magallanes would save you. He is weak. He cannot stomach harsh penalties.

Pah! Clubfoot showed no spirit. I truly believe that had we spat in his face he would scarce have dared raise a 'kerchief to wipe the spittle away."

Suddenly Cartagena's face hardened, and he leaped over and grabbed my arm. He squeezed so hard I clenched my jaw to keep from crying out. "Do not disappoint me, boy. Remember, though you now serve aboard the *Trinidad,* I am still your captain. I can slit your throat as easily as a rat's." He shoved me away. "Now be off, and remember what I said."

As I trudged up the *Trinidad*'s gangplank with my possessions, my heart sank. Espinosa was waiting for me, his arms crossed. No doubt he had heard what had happened at the council meeting. That I was a liar. A spy. Not to be trusted.

"Well?" he said after I put down my things.

I hesitated, remembering Cartagena's words: *I can slit your throat as easily as a rat's.* I looked away, hating Cartagena for making me lie. "It was an accident."

"Tell me, Mateo, how is spying an accident?"

I shrugged. "I don't know."

"Do you make a habit of spying?"

"No."

Espinosa was silent. I heard his breathing. The scrape of his boot against the planks. Then, "When I first met you at the inn, I felt you were a boy to be trusted. But maybe I was wrong. Tell me truthfully, young Mateo, and do not lie to me. Are you to be trusted?"

Are you to be trusted? With his words, tears filled my eyes. I blinked. It was a while before I could speak, and even then, my voice shook. "Upon the graves of my parents, you can trust me. Please—please believe me."

Espinosa gripped my shoulder. "Then look at me."

I did.

The ice blue of his gaze pierced me, as if he could see my bones. Read the truth upon my marrow. And the lie. I realized I was shaking but dared not look away. Then, abruptly, with a grunt, he turned and left, disappearing into the shadows of the quarterdeck.

"What was that about?" Rodrigo had come up the gangplank behind me.

I sighed and ran my hand through my hair. "I don't know, Rodrigo. Maybe they will kill us after all."

Rodrigo stared after Espinosa. Then he yawned and stretched. "Well, if they do, we should get some sleep first. Come on. Let's find a place."

That night aboard the *Trinidad,* I dreamed a terrible dream.

Through waves of dusty heat, a horseman appeared. He was a fine noble—fair-haired, blue-eyed, haughty. "I've come for my daughter," he said.

Out of the shadows of our home my father strode without a trace of limp—rugged, dark, angry.

My chest swelled with pride. My father. Tomás. "You may not have her," he replied, crossing his arms in front of his chest. "She is my wife. The mother of my son."

The nobleman spat. "Pah! What kind of life is this? Naught but toil and dirt. And you are naught but a filthy peasant. Give her to me now before I run you through."

"Never. She does not want to leave."

Then the sun flashed off a mighty lance as it thrust downward,

downward, from a great height. My father did not move. The lance pierced him through, blood spurted, and he slumped to the ground.

I screamed and awakened. Sweat dripped from me and I trembled, remembering.

I had dreamed this dream many times. But now it was different. Always before the lance had pierced my father's leg, leaving a great, gaping wound that caused him to limp forever. This time my father's very life had been struck down.

And that was not the only difference. As the tall nobleman had peered from his horse at the slain peasant, his face suddenly transformed into one I recognized. Cartagena's.

And the peasant who lay sprawled in the dirt with blood smeared on his face, over his deadened eyes, was no longer my father, but Magallanes.

The armada weighed anchor and put to sea bearing southwest. All ships followed the lantern of the *Trinidad,* the ship to which Rodrigo and I were now assigned.

I served as cabin boy for Magallanes. I could not bear to meet the captain-general's gaze, for I knew what he thought of me—that I was both a liar and a spy—and I was filled with shame. During my watches, I swept the floor, aired his bedding, turned the sandglasses every half hour, polished the woodwork, opened the window hatches, and brought him his meals, all with my head hanging, my gaze glued to the floorboards.

That evening, my watch over, I stood beside the bulwarks gazing at the multitude of stars, thinking of home, thinking of my father and mother. Trying not to think of how Cartagena had used me. I heard a voice behind me.

"They are beautiful, are they not?" It was Magallanes. "Ofttimes when I am anxious, I gaze upon the stars and find peace."

I said nothing, my shame so scalding I could not speak.

"You see that cluster of stars? That is Perseus. In one hand he holds his sword, and in the other he grasps the severed head of Medusa."

I looked to where the captain-general pointed but, try as I might, saw neither sword nor severed head. The stars looked very much the same to me. But I nodded, wondering why he spoke to me. Me, a liar and a spy.

"And there you can see the constellation of Andromeda. It is fitting she is beside Perseus, for in Greek mythology, they were husband and wife. You have not heard of that legend? Ah, it is my favorite." Then to my surprise, Magallanes went on to tell the story of how Perseus slew the sea monster and rescued Andromeda. Afterward, the captain-general stood silent, gazing at the stars.

Just that morning, after we were assigned our stations as cabin boys, Rodrigo had ridiculed me, saying I was cabin boy for a pig, while he was cabin boy for the tough master-at-arms, Espinosa. Now I looked at Magallanes, at his dark eyes gazing at the stars, and knew Rodrigo was wrong.

Magallanes spoke without turning. "I have ordered a space cleared for you and your friend in the storage area between the main deck and the fo'c'sle. I would advise you take it, for there are few places on this ship that remain dry in rough weather." At that, he left me.

I wondered. If Magallanes thought me a liar and a spy, then why did he care enough to find me dry quarters? Why did he speak to me, a mere cabin boy, pausing long enough to point out the constellations? And why was I not punished for spying? Had Espinosa talked to him about me? If so, what had Espinosa said? I did not know the answers to these questions, only that I slept soundly that night. I am Mateo, I thought dreamily, Mateo Macías of the *Trinidad*.

I did not carry out my duties alone. Magallanes owned a slave—Enrique—a man of dark skin, a man who never spoke, as silent as shadows. Sometimes I would think I was alone, sweeping, scrubbing, when suddenly there would be Enrique.

Rodrigo told me Magallanes had captured Enrique on one of his campaigns in the Far East when Enrique was a child. It had to be true. Enrique followed Magallanes like a dog follows his master. At first this bothered me, but soon I grew so used to it I scarce noticed him at all. Besides, I was glad to have someone else share my work.

For the next two weeks we sailed between the Cape Verde Islands and the African mainland, with blue skies and a steady wind from astern. There was some talk of this being a strange course the ships sailed, that perhaps Magallanes knew not how to sail a ship, much less navigate, but I did not listen to such talk. I trusted Magallanes in a way I had not trusted Cartagena. I could not explain it, but there it was. Each night as Magallanes paced the quarterdeck, silent and alone, his hands clasped behind his back, limping, I strummed my guitar under the stars, thinking of my father and wondering if he could see me.

Come dusk, whenever it was our watch, Rodrigo and I lit lanterns and hung them on the *Trinidad*'s stern so that the other ships could follow the *Trinidad* through the night. We also used the lanterns as signals in the event of storms, sandbars, reefs, or other deadly perils. Then, every night, after the lighting of the lanterns, each ship drew alongside, and one by one, the captains hailed Magallanes. "God save you, Sir Captain-General and master and good ship's company!" Magallanes acknowledged their salutes with a nod of his head.

And on each night as the *San Antonio* passed, Cartagena caught my gaze and held it, forcing me to turn away. How I hated him now. Each night I resolved again never to help him. Never. Even if he should slit my throat like a rat's.

Then, as we approached the equator, the weather changed. To the *Trinidad*'s stern I hoisted three lanterns. Headwinds slowed the ships until they no longer moved forward. They struggled and bucked like untrained animals under harness. We heeled so far to the sides our yardarms skimmed the waves and our curses turned to prayers.

One week passed and still the gales pounded us. Already I had fallen to my knees again and again, waiting to be swept overboard, to be swept to heaven, to my parents. Angry thoughts of Cartagena vanished like sea spray. The *Trinidad*'s bow rose to meet each wave, frantic, like an animal drowning, clawing for survival. Water crashed over the decks, tearing away anything not tied down. After each passing wave, the ship fell into the trough with a bone-crunching smack before rising with a shudder to meet the next wave. I clutched the railing and retched and retched alongside Rodrigo. He said we were "feeding the fish."

One night I burst from sleep as someone shook me with great violence. We are going down, I thought. It is the end.

"Mateo! Mateo!" It was Rodrigo.

Bleary, frightened, and exhausted, I sat up, then realized with a dull sense that we were not sinking. Rodrigo had awakened me for nothing. Angry, I pushed him away and lay back down.

"Read this."

"Leave me alone."

"Read this." He thrust a paper at me.

"What is it?"

"I believe it is the message from Spain, the message Cartagena told us to find."

"Where did you get this?" I grabbed it from his hand.

"From the captain-general's cabin while he was on deck. It was easy to find. You were blind not to see it. But I cannot read. You said you can, and now you must prove it."

I glanced at the paper, but it was too dark to see. Rodrigo followed me as we made our way aft, lurching to and fro as if we were drunk. No one paid us the slightest attention when I withdrew a paper from inside my shirt and held it near the lantern light.

The wind tried to tear it from my hand, and the driving rain splotched the ink. I shielded it with my body and read aloud.

Greetings, Captain-General Fernando de Magallanes,

In the name of the Most High and Mighty God Our Lord, I bring you warning. Take heed of the three Spanish captains from Castile: Cartagena, Mendoza, and Quesada. Before the fleet set sail, they openly boasted of slaying you. They despise you for receiving command of the coveted expedition and are supported in their hatred by the most powerful men in the Spanish court.

They conspire to replace you with that pup Cartagena, an untried weakling who has never before captained a ship, a weakling who will doubtless lead the fleet to disaster if given the opportunity.

Do nothing to arouse their suspicions.

Godspeed. Your father-in-law,

Diogo Barbosa

As I read the last line, a fierce gust of wind ripped through the ship. I allowed it to tear the letter from my grasp and watched as the parchment disappeared into darkness, swallowed by the raging ocean.

Rodrigo railed and called me a fool—a clumsy, bungling idiot with a brain no bigger than a turd—but it did not matter what he thought. I did not want him to give it to Cartagena.

Later, huddled beneath the fo'c'sle, we discussed the letter.

"I promise you, Mateo, Cartagena shall know about the letter, lost or not."

I snorted. "That will be quite a feat seeing as he is on one ship and you are on another. What are you going to do? Swim?"

Rodrigo glared at me, narrowing his eyes. "You mock me. You know I cannot swim any more than you can. Besides, there will come a day when we are once again on land, and it is then I will tell Cartagena everything."

"Everything?"

"Of course I will not tell him about how you tossed the letter overboard, unless you wish your throat slit. But I will tell him that Magallanes knows of his plot and to take heed."

"That is mutinous, Rodrigo! Cartagena is planning to murder the captain-general! You cannot possibly think of helping him!"

"Hopefully he will succeed. Then we will have a real man to lead the armada rather than this limping coward of a Portuguese."

"Magallanes is not a coward."

"What?" Rodrigo spat. "Are you blind? Did you not see the way Cartagena dominated the captain-general during the meeting? Did you not see my spittle on Magallanes's boot? Spittle that Magallanes did not bother to wipe away? It proves he is a coward. The whole ship knows it."

I nibbled on a fingernail. "I think he is a fine man." My words sounded uncertain.

"Pah! I think you are in love with him. Cartagena is a much finer captain than Magallanes. Any fool can see that."

"Cartagena has never captained a ship before. No more than I have. If he is captain-general, we will all sink and drown."

"What? Are you deaf as well as blind? Can you not hear the storm around you? You see, Mateo, the moment has already come when we will all sink and drown. All because of this lunatic. It is his fault. He has plotted a stupid course, into the path of a hurricane."

I pushed Rodrigo away and told him to leave me alone. And when he would not, I stumbled down the companionway into the hold and manned the pumps. Up, down. Up, down. Hour after hour, until my muscles screamed with pain. But I did not care. Anything to get away from Rodrigo.

Three days later, none of this mattered for we were about to die.

The storm lashed us, angry and hateful. We knelt about the padre to give confession, together vowing to pilgrimage to the shrine of Nuestra Señora de la Victoria, if we survived. Rodrigo and I waited and waited for our turn to confess but could wait no longer. The padre was too busy. We would die first. Pelted by rain, between peals of thunder and bursts of lightning, we clung to each other and hurriedly confessed. I to Rodrigo and Rodrigo to me.

"Forgive me, Rodrigo, my brother, my friend, for I have sinned. Yesterday I cursed my parents for dying of the pestilence—"

"That is nothing," he said, his face made eerie by a flash of lightning. "Today I cursed the stupidity of God and all His useless angels who sit with their wings folded, shining their golden halos while we die."

"Rodrigo!"

"It is true. Now His fury has been unleashed. Now we will all die. It is my fault, Mateo. Forgive me."

I gave Rodrigo much penance. I begged God to be merciful to his soul. Rodrigo did the same with me. Then, because we were not dead yet, I promised to give half my gold, my jewels, and my spices to furthering the work of God, should I live. Rodrigo promised a third.

Then in the distance a wave moved toward us. It was a wall of water, gigantic, towering like the castle walls of Castile. It came and it came, howling with the sound of death. We stood on the open waist deck, waiting. This was the end.

The ship rose, up, up, struggling to meet the wave.

Suddenly, to my bewilderment, strange green fires erupted from the rigging and the yardarms. I felt an odd tingling and my ears filled with a crackling sound. "We are saved!" Rodrigo cried, pointing to the green fires.

He threw himself upon the deck. I cast myself beside him. And beside me, the padre. "God has heard our prayers!" he yelled as the terrible, fearsome wave washed over us, tossing us hard against the scuppers, knocking the breath from me with the power of a sledgehammer.

Then the wave was gone.

Rodrigo coughed, spat out a mouthful of water, and crossed himself.

The padre wiped his eyes. "I have seen it before. It is the saint of sailors, San Elmo. While he protects us, none of us will die. It is a gift from heaven."

We dragged ourselves to our feet.

Then, while we watched, scarce believing our eyes, the saint disappeared. And with his disappearance, the clouds scattered, the sea grew calm, and a great multitude of birds settled upon the ship.

"It is a miracle," whispered the padre. "By the merciful hand of God, it is a miracle."

"Aye," I murmured.

There was no wind. No rain. No clouds. No waves. We hung our clothing from the rigging to dry and, for the first time in almost two weeks, sunned ourselves on the deck. I said the rosary again and again. Rodrigo and I no longer argued—a miracle, too.

But day after day passed without a whisper of breeze. The sea turned to glass, a liquid mirror in which I could see my reflection.

No one said it, but we all knew. We were becalmed, as help-less on the sea as a beetle on its back, frantically waving its legs, going nowhere.

So close to the equator, the air turned damp and stifling, crushing us, as if the *Trinidad* were no longer a ship but an oven, roasting us alive. The ship's wood creaked and swelled. My guitar was useless—its wood swollen with moisture, its tone flat as a puddle. I laid it aside. It did not matter. I could scarce breathe.

While the other captains rowed back and forth between their ships, visiting each other, the captain-general visited no one. Instead he paced the quarterdeck, hands locked behind him. He said nothing except to give orders.

Upon his orders, we polished the metalworks until they shone. While we slept, they rusted again, so the polishing never ended. Then the sails grew a green slime, nasty and rank, and each day we scrubbed for hours.

The water turned peculiar. It glistened like oil, and we feared to know what it was. And although there was not a wave in the ocean as far as we could see, the water swelled beneath us, lifting us up and up, twirling us around before dipping low again. The blocks rattled. The masts creaked and swayed. The yards slammed back and forth, making sleep only a dream. Men cursed each other and fistfights erupted like pox. The fights never lasted long. It was too hot.

Our rations for water, wine, and bread were cut in half. The meat turned rotten and stank. Casks of wine exploded in the hold, bursting their staves. The wheat shriveled into nothing but husks. Sharks swarmed about our ships. Espinosa caught one and cooked it and offered me a chunk. I hated the taste of its flesh. It tasted like dead men.

Normally we used a stern-slung cage as our latrine, but during the storms it had become too dangerous, tossing men about, and so we had used the bilges. Now a putrid vapor steamed from below, belching like a diseased bowel. It caught us unawares and the scuppers clogged with vomit.

We slumped in the shade, exhausted.

"Where has the captain-general led us?"

"Are we to die on this godforsaken sea?"

"Magallanes knows no more where he's going than a blind fish."

"It would be better if Cartagena were captain-general rather than this limping fool."

"I would sooner have the storms back and die in an instant than waste away until the birds pick the flesh from my bones."

Only Espinosa remained loyal, his face rugged and lined, his voice low yet as commanding as if he were on the battlefield. He said the next man who reviled the captain-general would find his privies skewered on the point of a knife and tossed to the sharks. That silenced the men. After that they waited until Espinosa slept or went to the latrine before again reviling the captain-general in hoarse, throaty whispers.

For myself, I knew not what to think. I knew only that I was sick with misery.

Even the ship sickened. Tar oozed from the seams. Water seeped through the timbers. We manned the pumps in the hold, panting, sweat pouring from us as the stifling heat sucked the marrow from our bones. Ten minutes was the longest anyone could pump. I hated the hold. I hated the pumps. I hated the raw blisters on my hands. But I hated the thought of drowning even more.

Two weeks after our misery began, clouds gathered. For a moment the pumps stopped. We gathered in the waist deck, breathless, waiting, hoping. The clouds opened, spattering us with hot, fat raindrops. After a few seconds, it was gone, and along with it our hope. We swelled with sticky moisture and despair, more miserable than before. Back we went to the hated pumps.

Then one day as I sat listless upon the deck, cursing the day I met Espinosa, I felt what I had not felt in weeks. A breath of wind.

It was almost a strange feeling, as if it did not belong. I raised my head. Did the others feel it, too? We looked at one another, startled. Then, above my head, the sails rippled. I slowly rose to my feet. Across the water I saw the sails of the four other ships snap, then billow, then tighten.

I raised my arms as a gust of wind blew the hair from my face, as the clouds opened with a burst of rain, sweet-smelling and cool.

Then Rodrigo was beside me. Naked from the waist up, we looped our arms and danced—laughing like children, whooping like savages.

After we crossed the equator, our troubles began anew.

Each evening Magallanes waited on the quarterdeck for each ship's salute. But on this night, Cartagena's ship, the *San Antonio,* kept her distance, the large ship mocking us with each dip of her bow. Cartagena stood on the quarterdeck with his dogs, smiling at the captain-general across the waters. Finally Magallanes left the quarterdeck, saying nothing, doing nothing, his hands linked behind his back as he limped to his cabin.

"Coward!" muttered Rodrigo to his back.

I could not meet Rodrigo's eyes. Perhaps he had been right all along. Any honorable man would demand retribution at such an insult. If it were me, I would have leaped across the space between us and impaled Cartagena on the point of my sword . . . if I had a sword.

Whispers spread among the crew like fire in the wind. *What does this mean? Such open defiance. Did you see the way Cartagena looked at him? Is our captain-general a coward?*

Then Rodrigo did something foolish. He told someone about the letter. Within minutes, everyone knew. . . .

Cartagena plans to kill Magallanes!
Did you hear?
Cartagena plans to kill Magallanes!

Again, the next night, the same thing. Cartagena refused to salute. And again. How much longer would Magallanes allow this to continue? The very air seemed to shout, "Our captain-general is a coward!"

On the third night, as stars clustered in the heavens like shells on the shore, the small ship *Victoria* pulled abreast and gave her salute. Captain Mendoza, one of the Spanish captains, then shouted, "Captain-General, sir, we have had an incident aboard." Mendoza paused and I could have sworn his face colored under the light of the lanterns. "Our master was caught, how shall we say—flagrante delicto—in the arms of his lover, an apprentice seaman."

On each ship, the master was second in command to the captain. To accuse the master of such a crime brought immediate silence to the *Trinidad*'s crew. We had all been warned. This crime, described to me in repulsive detail by Rodrigo, was punishable by death. I crossed myself and saw the movement of other arms in the darkness.

Magallanes sighed, and his face seemed to sag even more. "Very well. I shall arrange a court-martial with all captains and pilots for the morrow."

VII
November 24–25, 1519

The *Trinidad* hummed, vibrating like the strings of my guitar. It was the hum of voices, of cautious whispers.

"The Spanish captains could not have asked for a better opportunity," whispered Rodrigo later that night as a group of us crouched under the fo'c'sle. "At the court-martial, they will spring their trap."

I glanced around the circle of shadowed faces, remembering the letter, knowing Rodrigo likely spoke the truth.

Rodrigo continued, "Cartagena will simply stab Magallanes with his knife. It will be as simple as—as—well, I don't know. But it will be simple. I can tell you that."

"But the penalty for mutiny is death," I reminded him.

"Only for the loser, Mateo."

"Ah, don't be so reckless." A sailor stabbed his finger into Rodrigo's chest. "For whether you live or die depends on which side you choose. So choose wisely. It might be the last choice you ever make. As for me, I shall choose Magallanes, for the power of Espinosa and the marines lies behind him."

The men in the circle grunted in agreement. But I could smell the uncertainty. Even from Rodrigo.

During the night someone shook me awake. It was Espinosa. He held a lantern and his face glowed with an eerie light. Beside me, Rodrigo leaned on one elbow, his hair disheveled.

"No doubt the court-martial is a trap," Espinosa said, handing each of us a dagger. "I've arranged for the two of you to serve the wine and refreshments. It will be your duty to protect Magallanes."

I fingered the dagger, remembering how I had been caught spying, how Espinosa had questioned me afterward. Then you do trust me, I thought. But what about Rodrigo? Do you also trust him?

I glanced at Rodrigo. His face was masked and his eyes slitted.

Espinosa seemed not to notice, his voice heavy and grim. "I tell you, I would fill the cabin with marines if I could, but then the Spanish captains would not dare enter for fear of their lives. But the moment the door closes behind the Spanish captains, my marines shall be outside, ready to enter. Even now, they await my command. Naught shall come of this if we are prepared."

I did not admit my fear. I merely nodded, stuffing the dagger in my waistband under my shirt, feeling the press of cold steel against my skin. Until morning then.

The court-martial was swift and brutal.

Death. To be carried out once the fleet reached the shores of Brazil.

Upon hearing the sentence, the master stood immovable, while his young lover, a pimply boy with darting eyes, screamed and crumpled to the floor. "Have mercy!" he shrieked. "In the name of the Blessed Virgin, have mercy! I don't want to die!"

Four marines entered the cabin and hauled them away. Long after the door closed behind them, the shrieks continued, "Mercy! Mercy!" until the captains and pilots shifted in their seats. Then came a thud and an animal grunt. Then silence. A silence that lingered like death.

From across the room I saw Cartagena stare at Magallanes, unblinking. Behind him stood Rodrigo.

Magallanes cleared his throat. "Shall we continue? We have much to discuss and the hour grows late. There is still some confusion over the evening's salute. Perhaps we should review it again."

Cartagena yawned loudly. He propped his booted feet on the table and leaned back, looking disdainfully bored while the captain-general outlined proper procedure of the salute. When Magallanes finished, Cartagena heaved a sigh, removed his feet from the table, and said, "Finally. On to more important matters. There is still some confusion over the proper route agreed upon at the last council meeting. Perhaps we should review it again."

Magallanes seemed unperturbed. "As you wish."

I poured more wine while the captains and pilots spread charts upon the table, pointing and murmuring.

A nervous atmosphere pulsed through the air, tense and waiting. I met Rodrigo's gaze across the cabin. He looked away.

I scanned the room, my hand sweaty, itching to grasp the hilt of my knife.

Mendoza, captain of the *Victoria* and one of the three captains named in the letter, observed Magallanes with small, watchful eyes. Balding and stout, he groomed his beard with stubby fingers, each laden with a jeweled ring that flashed in the candlelight. Occasionally, he spoke a word or two, but mostly he watched the captain-general. It seemed to me his eyes grew smaller as he did so; perhaps it was a trick of the light, but I stood behind him anyway for I did not trust him.

Opposite Mendoza sat Captain Quesada of the *Concepción,* a man younger than Cartagena. He was monstrous and pale, his bull-like neck corded with blue veins. Hair the shade of alabaster flowed past his shoulders, and he stared at Magallanes with eyes of winter, as if he were sculpted not of flesh and bone, but of marble. The letter had warned against Quesada, and I knew that he, like Mendoza, would side with Cartagena.

But the letter had not mentioned Serrano, captain of the smallest ship, the *Santiago.* He, too, was Castilian. As I observed him, I wondered where his loyalties lay. He was the oldest of all the captains, older even than Magallanes. Unlike Quesada's face, which was cold and hard, Serrano's was soft and rounded, as if so many years of service had worn him down.

Now, with the pilots and various others, the captains hunched over the charts. Cartagena's comments, quiet at first, grew louder and louder. He glanced at Mendoza and Quesada as if gathering courage. "We would now have reached Brazil but for the bungling course chosen by the captain-general."

Again, the silence.

Magallanes shrugged. "Perhaps."

"If you had listened to me, we would not have spent two weeks caught in a gale, nearly losing our lives, and then three cursed weeks becalmed, wasting precious time and supplies." Cartagena began to strut around the room. On his head perched a feathered cap, the brightly colored feather as haughty and gloating as Cartagena himself. "And tell me, mighty Captain-General, since you know all there is to know, what will we do once we reach Brazil? For all this time you have refused to disclose the route you plan to take. It is knowledge that until now you stubbornly have kept to yourself, but it is time to share it. After all," Cartagena paused and glared at Magallanes, "what if something unfortunate were to happen to you?"

There followed a silence. All stared at Cartagena and Magallanes. I reached into my shirt and grasped my dagger. I shall strike Mendoza first, I thought, realizing blankly that I had never before raised a hand against another human being. My heart hammered in my chest. I blinked sweat from my eyes.

Finally, Magallanes raised his hand limply. "I beg your forgiveness, but I cannot share that information with you."

"I demand to know. Is there a secret passage through the southern continent?"

Magallanes cleared his throat. "I must apologize, but as I said, I cannot share that information with you."

Cartagena's face deepened in color, as scarlet as the feather. "And why, pray tell, can you not?"

Magallanes sat back in his chair and sighed. "I have shared my intended route with King Carlos, and knowing the route, he authorized the expedition. That should be enough."

Cartagena's mouth fell open. "Enough?" He laughed. A harsh, ringing laugh. "Enough? To know that the king, a feeble, pale boy of nineteen, a boy scarce strong enough to hold up his head, much less his crown, has agreed to your secret route? Pah! His chin is so large he can scarce chew properly or even close his mouth. A fly could penetrate the king's lips without difficulty! Of course he would agree to any folly! He is a moron. No doubt if you planned to sail your ships over dry land, he would applaud your genius. Ah, the great Magallanes has done it again. He has reached the Far East by sailing westward over a vast continent whereas all other men who walk the earth must sail east around Africa's Cape of Good Hope. He has snatched the spice trade from Portugal's greedy fingers and delivered it to the king of Spain. Once again, he has achieved the impossible!"

Cartagena's voice hardened and he pointed to the other men. "But we, Captain-General, are not untried fools of nineteen. We are men who follow you on a dangerous voyage, and we demand to know! Is there, or is there not, a secret passage?"

Magallanes brushed his dark beard and said nothing.

Cartagena stood before Magallanes. He gazed about the room, pausing in turn to look at each of us. "You see this man before me? He is nothing." Cartagena spat. "I will no longer obey the orders of a fool like Magallanes!"

Suddenly, the captain-general sprang from his seat, grasped Cartagena by the front of his shirt, and slammed him into the bulkhead. *"¡Sed Preso!"* he hissed.

Shaking with fury, Magallanes pulled Cartagena's surprised face down until it was level with his own. "You have insulted me for the last time, Spaniard. Your insubordination has been witnessed by these men. By rights, I can order you killed. Here. Now."

Cartagena's eyes widened. He licked his lips with a quick dart of his tongue. "Quesada, what are you waiting for, you idiot fool! Seize him!"

Quesada flushed and his pulse throbbed in the blue veins of

his neck. But he sat rooted, motionless. Behind him, Rodrigo paled, and I saw indecision in his eyes.

Cartagena turned to Mendoza. "Mendoza, seize him, I say! Now is the chance we have been waiting for! It is three against one!"

In front of me, Mendoza said through clenched teeth, "You are a fool, Cartagena." And he turned his head away.

"Indeed," said Magallanes, spitting his words into Cartagena's face. "A fool. You have just admitted to plotting mutiny."

Cartagena turned white. "But—I—I—"

Magallanes barked an order and the door flung open. Espinosa and his marines crowded into the room. "Arrest Cartagena for mutiny. Put him in the stocks."

Four marines grabbed the struggling Cartagena. "I did not mean it the way it sounded!" he cried. "Please!" His face was no longer the face of a proud Castilian captain, but the face of a frightened young man. "It was a mistake! Forgive me! Captain-General, forgive me!" As the marines pulled him through the door, Cartagena's feathered cap dropped to the floor.

VIII
November 25–December 22, 1519

Ha!

I laughed to see Cartagena in the stocks, his head and hands thrust through the openings as if he were a common sailor punished for swiping a hunk of cheese. Standing with my arms crossed, I gloried to see him brought low, to see him looking away from *me* for once, unable to meet my gaze.

"Are you crazy? Are you completely insane?" Rodrigo asked me later, grasping the front of my shirt with his fist. "Remember the words *Choose wisely?* Cartagena is not a man to make your enemy. I hear he is the son of the most powerful bishop in Spain. I tell you, if you make him angry, Cartagena will not hesitate to kill you."

"That would be incredible, since he is in the stocks and cannot move." I tried to pry off Rodrigo's hand, but he refused to let go.

"You laugh, Mateo, but this is not funny. You are an idiot if you think Cartagena will be in the stocks forever and a double idiot if you think there are not men who will do his bidding at the snap of his fingers."

His words rang true and I grew suddenly alarmed. I did not go around Cartagena anymore and felt only a grim relief when I learned he was stripped of his captaincy. On the *San Antonio*, his flag was lowered and the flag of a new captain raised to take its place. It was whispered that only his father's high position as a bishop had prevented an execution.

With Cartagena in the stocks, the fleet hoisted every scrap of sail and made good speed to Brazilian waters. On the sixth day of December the crew of the *Trinidad* burst into cheers when a brightly colored land bird settled on the quarterdeck railing.

All the next day, I smelled the scent of land. Rodrigo said it was the fragrance of jungle. I awakened the following day to the cry "Land ho!" We had been eleven weeks at sea.

For five days we hugged the coastline and headed south. We dared not land, for this part of Brazil belonged to the Portuguese and we feared for our lives lest we fall into their hands. From the railings we watched as the land rolled by. Monkeys swung from tree to tree. Flocks of parrots sprang into flight, clouds of red, green, yellow, and blue. Insects swarmed aboard, buzzing and biting.

"Do you think we will ever find a secret passage?" I asked Rodrigo. "Someone told me that the southern continent stretches both north and south forever and that it is impossible to go around."

"If no such passage exists, then this will be a short voyage. Unless we can sail over the jungle, that is." Rodrigo walked away, muttering, "Only a Portuguese would think of sailing west to reach the east."

On the feast day of Santa Lucia, when the heat smothered us

61

like fires from a blacksmith's forge, we anchored in a bay surrounded by lush hills. Once ashore, I fell to my knees and crossed myself. It began to rain, a great rain that made my hair hang in strings. Beside me knelt Rodrigo, and for the first time in many days we smiled at each other.

Crowds of natives swarmed the beach.

We stared at one another. The natives and we, the men from across the sea. We stared while the rains poured and the dirt beneath us turned to mud.

I stared at the women. How could I not? I had never seen a naked woman before. And there were hundreds of them. All naked. Beautiful and naked.

"Paradise," whispered Rodrigo, his eyes huge. "We've landed in paradise."

Trade began immediately. One of our men served as interpreter. A king of clubs or a queen of spades bought seven pineapples, a fruit both sweet and sour at the same time. A mirror bought ten chickens and two geese. A handful of beads bought a basket of fresh fish. Once it was discovered the native men had no metal tools, a hatchet bought one woman. If the sailor was lucky or the daughters especially ugly, one hatchet bought two. Trade was very brisk. Many men left their chores and could not be found.

Rodrigo gave me ten small bells to trade. Going into the village, I bought a shell necklace from a sag-breasted old woman who had but two blackened teeth in her mouth. She followed me around then, laughing behind her hand, pinching my backside if I turned away. I bought other things, too—pineapples, sweet potatoes, and a basket to store them in—meanwhile always followed by the old woman. Later, she sat staring at me, giggling as if I were the most hilarious thing she'd ever seen, as I spent the rest of the day drawing in my sketchbook. I sketched her as well. She would make a fine addition to my collection.

When I returned to the *Trinidad* and Rodrigo saw my purchases, he laughed and called me a weakling, asking why I did not buy myself a woman. I shoved him to the deck. "I am not a weakling!" I yelled. We fought until his eye was blackened and my ribs bruised, until we both lay on the deck panting.

The natives lived together in long houses called *boii,* each housing more than one hundred people. The next day, the old woman yanked me inside and proudly showed me their fire pit while tugging me toward her bed, a netting stretching from one log pole to another. I heard soft giggling and noticed a group of young women watching me. I flushed to the roots of my hair. Wrenching my wrist from her grasp, I backed out of the *boii,* smiling and bowing like an idiot while fending off her pinching, groping hands. Giggles erupted into laughter. Horrified, I fled back to the ship and said nothing to anyone, especially not Rodrigo.

On the twentieth day of December, the master of the *Victoria* was executed. All ships' companies assembled. The master stood tall. He looked at no one, said nothing, as Espinosa removed his shackles.

Once, when I was very young, I had seen a public garroting. I had forgotten the horror. The master was led to a post in the ground. To the post was attached a metal collar, which Espinosa affixed around the condemned man's neck. Espinosa turned screws on the garrote and the collar slowly tightened.

The master gazed above our heads, toward the heavens. His

eyes began to bulge. His tongue protruded, turning blue. I stood there, admiring his courage.

It was over. The master was dead.

The pimply-faced boy was not to be executed. He had appealed the sentence of death, saying the master had forced him. I despised him for his weakness.

One night, in a secluded clearing between palm trees, I played my guitar around a fire with Rodrigo and some other cabin boys. Because there was much joking and laughing between us, it was some time before we realized we were being watched. When we turned to investigate, the bushes rustled and we heard a chorus of giggles. Immediately my friends sprang to their feet and dashed into the bushes. There followed a great commotion of giggling. Of chases that crashed through the underbrush. Of shrieks and laughter. Then silence.

I sat alone before the fire. Why, I asked myself, why do I not follow? I knew the answer. I was afraid. Never before had I been with a woman. I grew angry and said to my feet, Take me into the bushes. Find a native woman.

But my feet would not move.

Then I heard a noise, quiet as a whisper of wind in the sails. A young woman, younger than I, slipped into the circle of light and sat upon a rock. Her brown eyes stared at me shyly. I stared back. Like the other natives, her skin was bronze-colored. Intricate designs swirled over her body, designs painted beneath her skin. She was tiny, slender. Her long black hair shimmered in the firelight.

She began to talk, but I could not understand. Then she laughed, a soft laugh like the tinkle of water poured from a jug.

The next thing I knew, she was sitting beside me and her hands were upon my face—stroking my cheeks, touching my lips. I caressed her smooth cheeks with trembling fingers. Her lower lip was pierced with three holes threaded with round pebbles. I traced the holes, wondering if it hurt. Then she laughed and I laughed with her.

Her name, I learned, was Aysó.

Sitting there that evening, she taught me a few words of her language, and I taught her to say *boy* and *song* and *girl* and *love*. I played my guitar and sang to her. I tried to teach her to play the guitar, my fingers clasped over hers. We laughed at her fumbling attempts. I showed her my sketchbook and then drew a picture of her. After she saw my drawing, she looked at me in amazement. I read her some of my mother's poems while she caressed the paper, nodding and smiling.

It was late before I left, the other cabin boys long gone. I dreamed of her that night, dreams soft as her skin and shining as her eyes.

The next day I rushed back to the same spot. My heart leaped when I saw she had returned. She smiled. "I'm back," I said happily, knowing she could not understand. We played the guitar and sang and drew pictures in the dirt, each of us talking, wondering if the other could understand. "Ship," I said, tracing the *Trinidad* in the sand. "Ship," she replied.

It was late afternoon when, after eating some fruit together, she took my hand and began to lead me through the jungle. "Aysó? Where are you going? Where are you taking me?" A wave of giddy happiness rushed over me and I thought, It does not matter. I would follow you anywhere.

After a while I realized we walked a trail. A tiny thread of earth snaked up the side of a mountain. We walked a long time, our hands entwined, no longer talking. We pushed gigantic leaves aside and stepped over branches and fallen logs. Frogs chorused and butterflies danced just out of reach. We crossed creeks, leaping from stone to stone, giggling when I slipped in the mud.

Suddenly there it was. A waterfall. It tumbled from a rock cliff and cascaded into a pool of water below. Water misted the air in a rainbow. Aysó slipped into the pool and then swam under the waterfall, beckoning me to follow.

"I cannot swim," I said, hungering to follow her.

When she motioned again, I could no longer resist. I turned away from her to undress, knowing it was ridiculous. Aysó never showed embarrassment over her nakedness. But I had never been naked in front of a woman, even if it was just for a swim. Had Rodrigo ever felt this shy?

Covering myself with my hands, I crept over the rocks and waded into the pool, going deep as quickly as I could, hoping my face was not as red as it felt. To my relief, the water was only chest-deep. Water rained on my head, streaming down my face, into my eyes and mouth. I spit out water, laughing, and when Aysó laughed, too, I pulled her toward me. "Waterfall," I said, pointing up.

Then, to my surprise, she reached up and pressed her lips to mine. Her lips, so soft. She tasted like rainbows of mist. My body melted into her kiss. My heart thundered. But when I tried to wrap my arms around her, she slipped away, under the water. "Aysó, come back!" My voice echoed through the jungle and up the cliff. Birds scattered from nearby treetops.

Now she was in the middle of the pool, laughing, shaking water from her long black hair. You are so beautiful, I thought. Just as I neared her, she dove, gliding past me under the water. I tried to catch her, but she slipped away, nimble as a dolphin.

It became a game. Each of us laughing, breathless, joy bubbling within me like fresh rain. Whenever she surfaced, I lunged after her, hoping to catch her, to kiss her. On and on we played for what seemed hours, until Aysó pointed to the sinking sun.

I sighed.

It was time to return.

Later, as we arrived at where I'd left my guitar and things, a new and surprising warmth overwhelmed me. It is love, I realized. My heart bursts with love. "You are so beautiful, Aysó. You make me so happy. I—I love you." I took her hands in mine, my heart racing, hoping she understood.

Aysó brushed her lips across my cheek. "Waterfall," she whispered in my ear. Then she was gone.

"I love her," I told Rodrigo that night as we lay on our bedding aboard ship.

"It is what we all think with the first one. Do not worry. It will pass."

"But I am serious. I truly love her."

"I believe you. You truly love her until you meet the next pretty native."

"Pah! Why did I even think you would understand?"

"Believe me, Mateo, I do understand. It is you who are brainless."

"If you understood, you would not speak to me so. If you understood, you would agree that I am really in love."

"Truly, Mateo, sometimes I think you are the stupidest person alive. What good is love on a voyage like this? You will only have to leave her."

"You are a liar, Rodrigo, and I will never talk to you again."

"God be praised."

I rolled over, pulling the blanket over my head, hating Rodrigo for always speaking the truth.

* * *

We sat beneath the full white moon, the fire blazing beside us. I had played my guitar and sang so much, I despised hearing myself. But Aysó, dearest Aysó, whenever I stopped, she motioned for me to play again. So I played again. How could I say no?

She sat beside the fire on a bed of leaves, cross-legged, weaving a chain of flowers. Already she had woven one chain into a circlet, which she had placed atop her head. "Mateo," she whispered, smiling to herself, her brown eyes peeping shyly from beneath the delicate crown. "Mateo."

I sang her a love song. Already I had sung it, what? Eight times? Nine? I had composed it myself and thought it very good.

Eyes like water,
Lips like wine,
I drink your love,
Sweet love divine. . . .

Then her hand clasped over mine, stopping my strumming. "Mateo," she whispered again. My breath caught in my throat as she quietly, slowly, placed the circlet upon my head. I could smell her sweet warm breath. Then she gazed at me, and I swore I saw love in her eyes.

But when I reached out to caress her, she gently took my hand and placed it on the strings of my guitar. She pointed at my guitar and at me. "You want me to play? Again?" In answer, she rubbed my hand across the strings. I smiled at the sound it made.

And so I played and sang while she made circlet after circlet, draping them on her, on me, on my guitar. I grew weary, the scent of so many flowers intoxicating. I imagined myself as a bee, drunk on nectar. The night became a dream, hazy, as if I watched myself from far away as I sang and played and sang and played, dizzy with love. Finally, my eyelids drooped. I stopped playing, laying aside my guitar, expecting Aysó to protest. But she was not even listening.

Instead, she lay curled beside the now smoldering embers, asleep on her bed of leaves, surrounded by flowers. Embers snapped and the orange of firelight flickered across her face, etching her in softness. She looked like a painting, motionless on a canvas. I watched her for a long time, unwilling to end this moment. Then, quietly, I removed my dagger, took off my shoes, and lay down beside her, wrapping my arm around her waist, imagining us together forever.

She moved closer to me as the sweet scent of crushed flowers twined through my senses. Sleep pressed upon me. The last thing I remember was the whisper of her name on my lips, painted across my heart. *Aysó* . . .

There was a distant shouting in the jungle that night, but I pulled Aysó closer and heard her sigh before I fell back to sleep.

Waterfalls. Dreams of flowers. Lips like wine. Shy eyes beneath a crown of petals. . . . I rolled over, dimly aware that the jungle darkness receded, that the fire was cold. Birds chorused overhead. Then a squawking, louder, louder . . . a rustling. The birds flew away.

Suddenly, I was yanked to my feet by my hair. My scalp screamed with pain. My blood surged with shock. Aysó shrieked and clung to me before she was torn away. *My God, what is happening?*

Then a marine shoved his face into mine, his features vague and distorted in the early morning light.

My heart leaped into my throat. Sleep vanished in an instant. I saw the deep shadows of pockmarks and knew I was in trouble again.

"You, Dog-Boy, are in violation of a direct command from the captain-general!" Spittle showered my face, my eyes.

"Command? But—but—I—"

"We have been searching for you through the night! I have lost sleep because of you, Dog-Boy. Shore leave is hereby canceled. Report to the ships immediately to prepare for departure. We leave in a few days."

Another marine stood beside Pock-Face. He was black-haired, black-eyed, and hook-nosed, reminding me of a crow. I did not like the glint in his eyes as his gaze swept over Aysó. A chill ran through me.

"I—I—must gather my things," I said quickly, wanting to end this, to lead them away from Aysó, back to the waiting ships.

Pock-Face shoved me toward my shoes. "Hurry. The captain-general is waiting. You sore try his patience."

I sat to pull on my shoes, meanwhile watching the other marine out of the corner of my eye. From the moment they had found me, the crow-faced marine had not stopped staring at Aysó. Aysó seemed to sense his gaze, for she hung back now, her eyes saucers of fright, confused. Beside me on the ground, partially concealed with leaves, lay my dagger. Making no sudden moves, I grasped the hilt, shielding the blade under my arm. "I'm ready. Let us go." I stood and casually fetched my guitar, turning from Aysó as if she were only a thing to be forgotten, my heart crashing against my ribs for fear.

Then it happened. What I had been dreading.

71

"Take him back to the ship, Segrado," said Crow-Face. "I'll only be a few minutes."

Pock-Face, or Segrado, as he was called, loosened his grip from my arm, and I sensed his hesitation. That was my moment.

I dropped my guitar, whirled, dagger in hand, and attacked Crow-Face. "Run, Aysó!" I screamed as my dagger bit flesh.

The marine cursed. Surprise splashed across his face.

"Run, Aysó!" With one look at me, panicked and terrified, Aysó turned and disappeared into the jungle. I heard nothing of her escape. I knew only that she was gone.

An arm locked about my neck from behind. "Drop the dagger, Dog-Boy!"

When I did not, the arm tightened. A veil of blackness began to fall over my eyes, and the dagger slipped from my hand. Run, Aysó, I thought. Keep running and don't stop.

A fist slammed into my gut.

Again, and again . . .

I stood facing Espinosa.

His ice-blue eyes studied me.

Just a few paces away, Magallanes gazed out the stern windows, his hands clasped behind his back. I saw the tightness of his jaw, heard the deepness of his breath.

Motionless and suffocating, the captain-general's cabin was as feverish as Spain on a windless summer's day. Sweat soaked my shirt, clinging to my bruises, my aching ribs. My bloodstained hands were shackled behind me, and on each side of me stood the two marines. My accusers.

Failure to return to the ship when ordered, they said. Resisting

72

arrest. Attacking a marine with a deadly weapon. A flesh wound only, but one blade's width to the left, and Minchaca would be dead. I was a boy gone wild, they said, uncontrollable.

When the accusations dwindled under the punishing silence, Magallanes turned. His dark eyes gazed at me, his brow furrowed. And although his eyelids drooped and the flesh beneath his eyes sagged, his stare pierced me like an arrow. For you, Aysó, I thought, my heart fluttering even now with the memory of her.

Under their scrutiny—Espinosa's and Magallanes's—I lowered my head. Shame covered me like a heated shadow, even though I had done nothing for which to be ashamed.

"Well?" asked Magallanes finally, waiting for me to answer.

I said nothing. Fearing to speak, fearing not to speak. From outside I heard the cry of a parrot. A dog barking. Laughter.

Then Espinosa said, "Leave us."

I looked up, surprised. *Leave us?*

"Segrado, Minchaca, both of you, leave us. Wait outside the door. The captain-general and I wish to speak to the boy alone."

I sensed their reluctance. But, like well-trained soldiers, they obeyed the master-at-arms, latching the door behind them.

Now I was alone with Magallanes and Espinosa. And even though I again looked at nothing but the boards in the floor, sanded and polished, I knew they regarded me. That they wondered what to do with me. That for the second time I faced the captain-general accused of a crime. That for the second time I shamed him. That he still believed me a liar and a spy. Perhaps Espinosa was regretting the day he'd stopped at the inn. That he'd shared his rabbit stew with me. . . .

"Well?" Magallanes asked again.

I sighed, miserable. "I had no choice," I finally mumbled.

"I can't hear you. Speak up."

"I had no choice."

"Every man has a choice, Mateo."

"Not me."

"I see. Tell me what happened."

"That marine, Minchaca. He was going to hurt Aysó."

"Aysó? Who is Aysó?" asked Espinosa.

"She is a girl. A woman, I mean." I felt myself flush.

"This Aysó, you were with her?" asked Magallanes.

"Aye, Captain-General."

"I see. And Minchaca?"

"The two of them came to take me back to the ship. But Minchaca wanted to stay behind. I knew he was going to hurt her." Now I looked at both of them. "I saw it in his eyes. Please believe me."

"Did he touch her?" asked Magallanes.

"No, but he was going to."

"Did he harm her in any way?"

Again I lowered my head, shaking it. It is useless, I realized. They will never believe me. For I am a liar and a spy and they no longer trust me.

"So you attacked him," asked Magallanes, "although he did not lay a hand on her?"

"Upon my word, Captain-General, he was going to. I told you, I saw it in his eyes."

Magallanes glanced at Espinosa, then sighed heavily. "You leave us no choice, Mateo."

"Aye."

He limped to the door and opened it slowly. Minchaca and Segrado stood at attention, waiting. "He is to have a dozen lashes, plus five days in the stocks. Minimum rations." Then he stepped aside as Minchaca and Segrado entered the cabin to take me away.

The next day was Christmas.

I heard the hymns. Heard the padre. Felt the movement of men around me. I endured their stares, heard their whispers.

A blackness deeper than I'd ever known suffocated me, greater even than the pain of my flogging. It was as if I were buried alive, dirt seeping into my ears, my eyes, my nostrils, my mouth. Weight crushing my chest.

Aysó was gone.

I was gone.

I knew I would never see her again, for the armada would move out to sea as soon as Christmas ended. Yet there was one bright spot I clung to, a golden lantern in a storm of blackness. Even though I would never see Aysó again, I had rescued her from Minchaca.

Aysó was safe.

I would cling to this forever, through all the storms to come, perhaps even death at the hands of monsters or cannibals, perhaps even dropping off the edge of the world. Aysó was safe.

Then, like the ocean at the change of tide, my thoughts turned again and my blackness deepened. I remembered both Espinosa and Magallanes. Their probing stares, their disappointment in me. The captain-general still thought me a liar and a spy, and yet this time I had done nothing wrong. It was not fair! Nothing was fair! I would have pounded my fist in frustration and rage, but the stocks held me tight, pinning me like a rat in a trap. And Espinosa? He had trusted me, brought me on this journey when I had nowhere to go, nothing to eat. Now I had sorely disappointed him.

I vowed to kill Minchaca. It was my right. My honor. He would be sorry for the day he laid a fist on Mateo Macías de Ávila!

Lost in my ocean of thoughts, I did not realize at first that someone was talking to me. "Mateo," the voice repeated, "I must speak with you." It was Espinosa. He squatted in front of me so I had no choice but to see him, then reached up with a muscular arm and brushed my hair from my eyes. I turned my face away. It was he who had flogged me the day before, afterward walking away without a word. I could not bear to look at him. What more was there to say? Were not a flogging and punishment in the stocks enough? Could he not see my shame? My rage? Did he not hate me now for disappointing him?

Then, before I could stop myself, I said, "I'm thirsty."

He returned with a cup of water. He held my head while I drank. It was difficult to drink, to throw my head back far enough. I could not use my arms, for they were locked in the stockade along with my neck. Water dribbled down my chin. Waves of pain pulsed through my back.

"I must know," whispered Espinosa. "Is it true? What you have said?"

I nodded. "Aye."

"You were defending a woman?"

"Aye. They beat me when I helped her to escape." I spoke through gritted teeth. "No matter what you think, I am not a liar."

"Mateo, you are too quick to judgment. The truth is, I believe you. I have always believed you."

I blinked, unsure of what I'd heard. "You believe me? Then why—"

"You must understand we had no choice. Punishing you was not a matter of friendship, but of duty and regulation. My opinion of you is beyond that."

Tears stung my eyes. "And the captain-general? Does he believe I am a liar?"

"Perhaps someday you should ask him."

"Then what about Minchaca?"

"What about him?"

"He violated the order not to molest native women—or at least he was going to violate it. Someday, in the name of honor, I will kill Minchaca. I promise you, he will beg for mercy."

Espinosa sighed. "Mateo, listen to me. I am your friend, right?"

I nodded.

"I am also master-at-arms, and Minchaca is under my command. You are to do nothing. Do you understand?"

Again tears stung my eyes. "But I must have my revenge."

"There is much of this voyage yet to come, Mateo. To have enemies is a terrible burden, especially for one as young as you. Trust me, and promise you'll do nothing."

I hung my head, torn. "I don't know."

"Promise me."

Then, like a dam that breaks, releasing the flood, relief washed through me and the darkness in my heart ebbed away. "I promise. I promise."

Espinosa squeezed my hand and left.

* * *

Rodrigo came to see me many times. He filled my ears with warnings, with rumors, with anything that crossed his mind. "Everyone is talking about you. Is it true that you were sleeping with ten native women? That when the marines tried to take you back, you attacked five of them with a sword? Is what they are saying true, Mateo? If it is true, then you are very brave. Very stupid, but very brave."

Later, "I have heard the most incredible thing, Mateo. I have heard that you stabbed Minchaca. Is that true? If it is, then you are a fool. You should know not to stab marines. Even so, I will finish the job for you. Just say the word, and it is done. You can trust me, my friend."

Then in the middle of the night I heard a rustling near me, and again, Rodrigo. "You see?" he whispered, slipping some fruit between my lips. "What did I tell you? You are a double fool, Mateo. A triple, double fool. Never, never fall in love with native women. That is the rule of sailors. You would not be in this position if you had taken my advice."

On the morning of the twenty-seventh, as the sun warmed my face, the crew of the *Trinidad* sang a chantey, circling the capstan. Muscles gleamed to the rattle of anchor chain. From the fo'c'sle came the cry "Heave and pawl! Get all you can!"

From the quarterdeck, "Lay out and loose!"

We were setting sail. Soon Brazil would be nothing but a memory. Rodrigo stood beside me, coiling a line, glancing over the gunwale. "Do you hear them, Mateo? The natives are crying for us. They have surrounded our ship with their canoes. I wish you could see it."

Indeed, there were many cries—men, women, even dogs barking and the wail of a baby. I strained my ears for the sound of Aysó's voice. Once more, just once more, I prayed.

Again from the quarterdeck, "Lay in and down from aloft!"

"You see, Mateo," continued Rodrigo, "the native men cannot compete with us Spaniards. The native women, they love us. We are the greatest lovers in the world. They don't want us to leave. The native men like us, too, because we give them things for their women. Nails, buckets, hatchets, things they cannot get otherwise. It is a fine situation all around. Everyone is saying we should stay. Everyone but the captain-general that is, and, well, you know how he is. Not even God could sway him otherwise." Rodrigo spat and hurried off.

"Man topsail sheets and halliards! Tend the braces!"

"Sheet home and hoist away topsails!"

The wind filled our sails, carrying us to sea. The cries of the natives grew dimmer . . . dimmer . . . finally scattering into the sounds of the sea. Nothing but the sea.

X
December 30, 1519–January 13, 1520

Each day the same. Scrub. Polish. Cook. Scrape. Sweep. It made no difference what I was doing, for each task seemed the same. Day after day. Watch after watch. I could not keep my mind on my chores, for I had no mind to keep.

"Always look sharp, Mateo," said Magallanes when I tripped over my broom, sprawling onto the floor of his cabin, stinging my chin.

"Aye, Captain-General."

Once when I accidentally kicked over a bucket of water, Magallanes said nothing, only shook his head and returned to his silent study of his charts.

Air his bedding. Wash his clothes. Roll up his charts and stow them when not in use. Fetch more candles. Turn the sandglasses. Swab the deck.

I was thinking of nothing one day when, again, I stumbled. A storm railed around us, and the *Trinidad* lurched through the swells like a drunkard. This time I had my hands full. I carried a wooden platter of food for the captain-general—dried fish, pickled meats, cheese, biscuit with marmalade—when I fell full into Magallanes, who sat at his table waiting for dinner. The platter landed on the captain-general's chest, while I stumbled against him, registering his look of shock before I bounced onto the floor, bits of biscuit and marmalade and pickled meats on my cheeks.

I lay there for a moment, stunned, my head reeling. "Sorry, Captain-General," I mumbled.

Even through the noise of the storm, I heard him sigh. "Clean it up, Mateo, and after this, have a mind for yourself. You've become a nuisance."

"Aye."

It took me an hour to clean it up. I helped Magallanes out of his soiled clothes and into clean ones. He noticed a stain on his clean tunic, scratched at it, and asked me if I hadn't just washed this a few days ago. "I can wash it again, sir," I replied.

"Never mind, Mateo." Again the sigh.

I scrubbed the table and the floor, tossing food scraps into the bucket. I fetched the captain-general another platter of food. I set the platter in front of Magallanes, placed the napkin on his lap, and poured him a goblet of wine. "Anything else, sir?" I asked, anxious to eat my own dinner.

Magallanes motioned to one of the chairs. "Please, sit."

"Sir?"

"That is, if you can do it without falling."

I flushed and sat as commanded.

For a while he said nothing, his beard wagging up and down as he chewed. A fierce gust of wind hit the ship, and she heeled heavily. With an automatic movement, Magallanes picked up the goblet, wine slopping, while the platter of food slid to his left, stopped from falling over the edge by wooden runners along the table's surface. "When I was a boy, younger than you, twelve I think, my family sent me to live in the court of the queen of Portugal. It was there I received my training as a page." The platter of food now slid to his right. Magallanes seemed not to notice and kept eating, moving from left to right with his food.

"The queen of Portugal?"

"I'm afraid I was a clumsy boy, always knocking something over, stepping on the ladies' toes, falling off my horse. Once I even spilled a pitcher of milk down the front of the queen's dress. It seemed I could do nothing right. I was always getting my ears boxed."

I tried to imagine someone boxing the captain-general's ears but couldn't. Such an image seemed as impossible as the Virgin Mary scrubbing out the bilges.

"All that changed when I went to sea."

"Sir?"

"You see, Mateo, sometimes a boy needs a vision. A dream. Hope. Something more than just what others tell him to do. For me, it was the sea." The wind gusted, howling like a pack of wild dogs. The timbers groaned and the *Trinidad* shuddered. Dabbing his mouth with a napkin, the captain-general said, "Come, Mateo, let me show you something."

I followed him across the cabin, my curiosity rising.

He opened one of the lockers and handed something to me. "What is it?"

"It's an astrolabe. A friend of mine made it from wood."

It was flat and round, with intricate carvings and movable pieces. Even knowing nothing of such things, I saw it was beautiful and felt honored he would let me hold it. "What is it for?"

"It tells me the altitude of the sun so I can calculate our latitude. On the next clear day, I will show you how it works."

"Aye, sir." I handed it back to him.

"Now, fetch your guitar and sing to me. After you've had your dinner, of course. That is all. And, Mateo—"

"Sir?"

"Please stay on your feet."

"Aye, sir."

As I opened the door to leave the cabin, one of the shadows breathed. Enrique, the slave. For some reason, I shivered. I had not even known he was there.

On every clear day after that, I held the captain-general's instruments as he measured the noon sun while explaining to me how they worked. I nodded, pretending to understand. Maybe, someday, I would know as much. Maybe, someday, I would also be captain of a ship. I then followed him to the poop, where he scanned the coastline of the southern continent as we journeyed ever southward.

Searching . . . always searching for the secret passage—*el paso*.

Each evening after dinner now, I played my guitar and sang for the captain-general—songs of battle, serenades of love, hymns of glory, ballads of sorrow. He seemed to want them all. He tapped his foot, closed his eyes. He wept, unashamed. He limped about the cabin, conducting an invisible symphony. He lay upon his bed, staring at the ceiling, his face sagging and blank.

Sometimes after my evening singing, we again climbed to the poop, where I unrolled his charts, holding them as his forehead creased in thought. He would point to a part of the chart, saying,

"Bring the lantern closer, Mateo. See? According to my calculations, we are almost there. I feel it. Any day." Then he would gaze into the darkness as if he could see our destination if only he looked long enough.

One day in mid-January, I was polishing the wood walls and dreaming of Aysó when Magallanes burst into his cabin. "Quick," he cried. "My charts!"

A moment later, he pounded the chart with his fist. "I have done it!" His dark eyes danced. "We are here! Mateo, do you hear me? We have made it!"

Caught up in his excitement, a smile stretched across my face, I helped him into his armor and his helmet with plumed feathers. "I must call a conference aboard the *Trinidad*," he was saying as he fastened his sword to his side. "This is a day of triumph! Do you hear me? Triumph! Praise be to God Almighty!" Then out he rushed like a brisk wind on a stormy day, leaving me with my silly grin and my rag still in my hand.

I hurried to finish the woodwork, anxious to learn why the captain-general was so excited. I ran out on deck. My breath caught. Slicing through the southern continent and disappearing into the horizon lay a vast westward passage. *El paso!*

Once all the officers had gathered on the quarterdeck, Magallanes cried, "Few men have stood where you stand now, on the brink of discovery. Have courage, my men, for what might lie ahead. We shall sail through this westward passage into a new ocean, into new waters never before sailed by man. Imagine being the first to reach the Spice Islands by traveling west!"

We glanced at each other as suddenly rumor became fact. It

was true! We were headed for the Spice Islands! Another paradise of riches and women! Rodrigo clapped me on the back. "What did I tell you? It was a lucky day we signed for this voyage."

"And in the name of King Carlos, I shall claim the Spice Islands for Spain!" cried the captain-general.

I could not stop grinning. As though I had led the armada myself. As though I stood before everyone, dazzling in a suit of armor, a shining sword at my side, as they honored my triumph. It is a good day, I thought. Soon we arrive at the Spice Islands and then we shall return to Spain with riches and glory.

By nightfall we had traveled more than seven leagues into the strait when we dropped anchor. Rodrigo and I stood at the bulwarks. Fires ringed the shores and the light of flames flickered on the dark faces of natives. There were hundreds of them—thousands even. The deep beat of drums pounded through my heart.

These were the natives who devoured the flesh of men.

Their screams pricked the night.

"You have heard the story?" whispered Rodrigo.

"What story?"

"About the foolish Spanish explorer who went ashore. The cannibals captured him and sixty of his men. They cooked and ate them while everyone aboard the ships watched. They could do nothing to save their shipmates."

"Is this true?"

"As true as we are standing here. They say the natives spitted and roasted some of them over hot coals. That the flesh turned black as a raven and fell from the bones like chicken meat. Others they stuffed into cauldrons and made people stew with intestines for noodles and eyeballs for olives."

Now the natives danced around their fires. They held up their weapons and screamed at us, as if daring us to come ashore. My scalp prickled. "I hope we reach the end of the strait soon," I said, chewing nervously on a fingernail.

"Aye." Rodrigo nodded. "It is difficult to become rich if we are sitting in a cauldron staring at our eyeballs."

The cabin was lit only by a sputtering candle. Magallanes lay on his bed, his eyes closed, his hands clasped across his chest. For a moment, he looked almost youthful.

He did not move when I began to sing.

It was my father's favorite song, and I hoped it would please the captain-general.

I sang of the apostle Santiago, of his sword burning bright as he cut down the infidels. I sang of the conquests of the Knights of Santiago—righteous men who covenanted to follow the apostle. I sang of four thousand mounted knights and five thousand footmen, each wearing his scallop shell to glorious victory against the Moors.

I sang until the eleventh verse, when I found I could not continue. It was not the words that caused me to falter, but Magallanes himself. As he lay on his bed, his hands across his chest, his eyes closed, he reminded me so much of my father that my music trailed off like a wisp of smoke.

Magallanes opened his eyes and studied me. I hoped he could not see the tears poised in my eyes, threatening to fall. I blinked them back and wiped my face on my sleeve. I wished he would dismiss me with a wave of his hand the way he usually did.

He did not. Instead he asked in a voice that surprised me with its kindness, "How old are you, Mateo?"

"Fourteen."

Magallanes sighed. "Espinosa told me about your parents. He said they are dead. I am sorry. You are young to be alone."

"You—you know?"

"Even before we left on our voyage, he pointed you out. Do you know what else he told me?"

I shook my head.

Magallanes propped himself up on his elbow. "That you were a good lad and to keep my eye on you, for you would do well on this voyage. That not only were you strong in body, but strong in character. Indeed, you do well to look surprised. Those are high words of praise coming from a man such as Espinosa. He does not waste words."

A question burned at my lips, one I had wanted to ask a dozen times. Nay, a hundred times. "Do you—do you really think me a liar and a spy?"

Magallanes frowned. "What do you mean?"

Now I fumbled for words, embarrassed, wishing I had not asked. "Minchaca and Segrado, you know, and—and that—that night at the council meeting when I was caught, you know—" My face heated with the memory. I looked away, unable to meet his gaze. What a fool I am! Now he will think me a liar, a spy, and an idiot besides!

"Mateo, on the night of the council meeting, when they first brought you before me, I knew not what to believe. I admit, I was angry. But there was something not right. Something was wrong, something foul, and I knew Cartagena was somehow involved."

Astonished, I stared at him. "You knew? You knew Cartagena ordered us to do what we did? That we had no choice?"

"Perhaps not entirely, but I knew enough to stay the hand of execution. It was not right that two boys should perish."

"But Rodrigo spat upon your boot!"

The captain-general's face darkened. "Aye. It took much control not to have him slain. But"—Magallanes smiled, and a faraway look stole over his face—"my own infant son is named Rodrigo. It would be an evil omen to stain the name with blood, especially if that blood be innocent."

My mouth hung open. I knew I looked idiotic but could not help myself. Magallanes had known! For all these weeks while I suffered from shame, always wondering what he thought of me, he had known! "Then what about the flogging and the five days in the stocks?"

He waved his hand. "Regulation, only—the standard punishment for resisting a marine. Also a lesson, perhaps, that a boy your age should know better than to get involved with native women. But no matter. It is finished, and I trust it will not happen again." He lay back and closed his eyes. "Sing me another song, Mateo. Sing until you can sing no more, for tonight, tonight I am triumphant."

XI

ℱebruary 2–March 31, 1520

"He is a stubborn man," said Rodrigo. "Portuguese and stubborn. Any fool with eyes and a grain of sense would realize this is not *el paso*. It is nothing but a river."

It was true. After several weeks of exploration, even Magallanes had to admit it. "Turn the ships around," he said, suddenly seeming years older.

Like Magallanes, I tasted bitter disappointment, as if my mouth filled with ashes. His triumph had turned to failure. What would we do now? What would Magallanes do now that he knew this was not the passage? Would we ever find the passage? Did such a passage even exist?

Back at the entrance, a conference was called. The captains and pilots urged Magallanes to turn east and head toward the Spice Islands by the known route, around Africa's Cape of Good Hope. "At least by that route we will arrive," they said. "At least by that route the expedition will not be a total failure. We will return with spices for the king."

The crew had other ideas. "Return to Brazil for the winter," they begged, I along with them, already feeling Aysó's warmth and her smooth skin. "When the weather improves in a couple of months, we can sail farther south and try to find the strait again."

The captain-general's face hardened. "We continue south now," he said.

The entire crew broke out in protest.

Beside me, Rodrigo spat and narrowed his eyes. "Here we go again," he whispered. "Like I said, Portuguese and stubborn. It was a sorry day I signed for this voyage."

"Silence!" barked Magallanes. "We shall go on!" Then his face softened. "Despair not, my friends. The strait is not here, but we will surely find it a few miles farther down the coast. We will sail through it and spend the rest of winter among the islands of the South Sea, where even the cooking pots are made of gold and the women surpass those of Brazil in beauty."

With that, Magallanes dismissed us. It was decided: we would continue southward.

"If Cartagena were our captain-general," mumbled Rodrigo as we prepared for departure, "we would be home by now."

"Dead, more than likely," I replied.

"Everyone except the captain-general knows there is no passage. He is a blind fool."

"How do you know there's no passage? Have you sailed down the coast and checked for yourself?"

"It is common knowledge."

"Common to whom?"

"It is what everyone is saying."

"They may say that, but they know nothing."

"If you are so smart, Mateo, then tell me what makes you think there *is* a passage, besides your stupid faith in the captain-general? If you ask me, you're the one who knows nothing."

As I hurried off to batten down Magallanes's quarters, my stomach tightened. Rodrigo is right, I realized. I know nothing. None of us know. Not even the captain-general.

Even before we had reached the entrance to the false passage, we were farther south in latitude than the Cape of Good Hope in Africa.

Cold winds gusted across our decks, whistling through the rigging, ripping the sails apart until they hung like rags. Sleet, hail—weather such as I'd never seen before—pounded us. Ice clung to the rigging, ghostly white. Mountainous waves tossed the ships like empty bottles. Sandbars, reefs, and rocky atolls lay beneath the surface like sea monsters.

The captain-general insisted we probe each inlet. Searching, always searching, for *el paso,* the passage to the South Seas. He paced the quarterdeck, limping, his clothes caked in ice, his hair and beard heavy with icicles. He crackled when he moved—we all did—and sometimes the ice dropped from his clothes, shattering like glass. Magallanes never slept more than four turns of the sandglass at once. And, like us, he never ate a hot meal. A hot meal was impossible—the winds blew out all shivering attempts to light a fire.

I slept with my rosary, with Rodrigo huddled beside me. Even between the fo'c'sle and the main deck, I suffered from cold. Waves washed over the decks, and I would burst from sleep, gasping, dreaming I was drowning.

For two hundred leagues we did not see another human being. It is not surprising, we said among ourselves, for who could live upon this desolate land? The shore was rocky and barren. We reeled through snowstorms in search of a harbor. It was not to be found. Reefs guarded the steep beaches. Waves half the height of our tallest mast crashed into the shores.

Everything I touched was frozen. My hands cracked and bled. I lost three fingernails. Rodrigo lost two. I was always wet, chafed, raw—like a piece of meat. Salt water made the chafing worse, causing sores that bled and oozed. I winced every time I moved.

And to our confusion, the days grew shorter as February turned to March. This was not supposed to happen. We did not understand. Surely the weather would improve and the days grow longer, for spring was fast approaching. Yet the farther south we went, the more the weather pounded our ships and flattened our hearts. It seemed winter would never end.

Thoughts of Aysó now seemed but a dream. A dream of something long ago. A warm dream that mocked my chilling nights.

One cheerless gray day, when the wind whistled in my ears until they screamed with pain, we anchored in a small bay, rugged and ugly, where the rocks jutted from the ground like bones. On the shore were strange animals that I had never seen before. As I brought out my inks, Espinosa approached. "Mateo, Rodrigo, come with me in the skiff. The captain-general has asked us to find wood and water."

Rodrigo and I rowed quickly, anxious to reach land.

We scraped bottom and jumped out. Immediately the animals erupted into an awful wailing, a barking almost. I clutched my dagger, ready to kill if one attacked. Up close they appeared ferocious and their teeth looked very sharp. Seawolves, we called them. They were fat, furred animals, forced to slither on the ground. Instead of legs they had a kind of hand, one on each side, which they used to propel themselves forward. Now they fled with a deafening noise, galloping away on their bellies, some flopping into the water. There was also a strange bird, a kind of black-and-white goose that waddled upright but did not fly. It had been a long time since I had tasted fresh meat and my mouth watered to see these animals.

It did not take us long to discover there was no wood or water ashore, at least none that we found. But before we could return to the *Trinidad,* a great storm arose.

Blinding snow peppered my eyes. The wind howled. We stumbled in the direction of the skiff, clinging to each other so we would not be separated. Espinosa, then Rodrigo, then me. I could see nothing. My hands, maybe. Or Rodrigo's shoulders. How could we return to the ship if we could see nothing?

It seemed forever that we stumbled about. My teeth chattered. My lungs ached. My nose and fingers grew numb. Surely we should have reached the skiff by now. Then Espinosa's face loomed out of the whiteness, ghostly, as if detached from his body. "We're lost!" he cried, his voice snatched away in the shriek of the wind. "We've been walking in circles! We must find shelter and wait out the storm! Follow me!"

My heart began to beat wildly. We staggered on. And through the whiteness I heard sudden movements, first here, then there. Seawolves. Perhaps the beasts would devour us.

And then we were there. A jumble of boulders, a cave almost. Espinosa disappeared into its center. Then Rodrigo. I entered and caught my breath. Masses of seawolves surrounded us. "We will shelter here," cried Espinosa. And while I fumbled for my dagger, my heart thudding, my ears filled with their barking, imagining their teeth sinking into me, he slaughtered four of them. The rest scattered, slithering out of the shelter. "Gather their warmth while you can!"

Cursing and sweating, the three of us pulled the bodies around us until we sat in their center, huddled together for warmth. Curls of steam rose from the carcasses. Blood pooled under me. It soaked into my breeches, my boots. "What now?" I asked, shivering.

"We wait until the storm ends," answered Espinosa, his breath steaming.

I gaped at him. "But some storms last for days!"

"Aye."

"But—but—" I stammered. "What can we do? We have no water. We have no food, unless, of course, we eat them . . . raw." I prodded the beast behind me.

Espinosa sighed heavily. "For now, you must stay awake. For in cold such as this, sleep means death."

"That's all?" I asked.

"Aye."

I glanced at Rodrigo. "It's your fault," I said. I was only half-joking.

Rodrigo scowled. "My fault? How can this be my fault?"

"Remember when we were about to die in that storm? I promised God one-half of my riches to further His work, while you promised only one-third. This is His vengeance."

"Pah! I always thought you were a fool, Mateo, and now I know it is true. Besides, that was a long time ago, before we even reached Brazil. If God wanted me dead, He would have killed me long ago."

I shrugged. "God is patient. He waited for the right time to punish you." When I saw a shadow of fear cross his face, I laughed. "I am teasing, Rodrigo. It is a joke."

"A poor joke."

"I thought it funny." I wrapped my coat as tightly around me as I could and moved closer to Rodrigo, leaning back against one of the carcasses. I could no longer feel my feet. Already they had turned to ice, sitting in pools of frozen blood.

"If you would like to hear a good joke," said Rodrigo a while later, his teeth chattering, "listen to this. Why does Magallanes keep wandering around?"

"I don't know."

"Because he is lost."

"That is not funny."

"Neither was yours."

The sound of the wind filled my ears. Cold crept through me until I could feel nothing, not my legs, nor my hands. All of us shivered uncontrollably. Even Espinosa.

Each hour, each minute, shrouded with ice. I tried to talk, to keep awake, but my mind kept wandering, and I found myself staring at nothing. Thinking nothing.

Sometime during the night, Rodrigo mumbled, "One-half. I will give one-half."

But I did not understand because a great heaviness pressed upon me and I grew sleepy, as if I were being sucked into the watery eye of a whirlpool. *Come, Mateo,* it beckoned.

Come . . . come to where it is warm.

. . . Blessed warmth.

Leave the cold behind.

. . . Heat. Stones. Ávila.

There is nothing for you here.

. . . Tomás. María.

Here you are alone.

. . . I am coming home.

Then a face leaned over me, and I heard a voice calling, "Mateo! Mateo! You must awaken!" Someone shook me again and again. Go away, I thought angrily. Leave me.

"You must fight it, Mateo! Awaken now before it is too late!"

Warmth slithered through me, pulling me down, away, away. *Come . . . come . . . ,* it whispered. *You need be cold no longer. You need no longer be alone. Come . . .*

No! I thought. No! I don't want to die! I want to live! Someday I shall return to Spain! Suddenly, like an arrow piercing my ribs, I became aware of pain—excruciating pain. My body shrieked with cold.

"Help me!" I cried, hot tears coursing from between my frozen eyelids.

I was dragged from the shelter. Seawolves scattered, barking. Thousands of birds took to the air, their wings thrumming like the beat of my heart. I blinked in the glare of sunlight, scarce able to stand. And I realized in that moment how close I had come to death. Espinosa had saved my life. I clung to him; I clung to Rodrigo, thinking, I am not alone.

"Come!" cried Espinosa. Together the three of us stumbled toward the shore.

At least fifty seawolves littered the beach, each dead in a bath of blood. Men skinned the carcasses. One of our shipmates looked up and saw us. "There they are! We've found them!"

They hurried to help us and we collapsed into their blood-soaked arms.

On the last day of March, a cleft opened in the coast. The entrance looked forbidding, but Magallanes ordered the *Trinidad* forward with a wave of his hand. After sliding over a bar, the ship's bottom scraping sand, we hove to in a bleak harbor, surrounded by towering cliffs.

Magallanes scanned the harbor. He sent Espinosa, Rodrigo, and me ashore. After we returned with a report of both fresh water and wild game, he said in a voice as stark as the shoreline, "I am pleased. We will stay here."

XII

March 31–April 2, 1520

Mutiny. . . .

It swirled around us like the wind. Merciless. Sweeping down from the plain and howling between the cliffs that encircled the bay. We stood onshore, surrounded by the stench of utter desolation.

Addressing the entire fleet's company, Magallanes ordered dwellings built.

In response there was nothing but silence. Silence, and that bone-numbing wind. Already my feet were frozen. Now, with a look of steel upon his face, as if smelted in a forge instead of a womb, he ordered rations cut immediately as a precaution.

A deafening cry arose.

"Take us back to Spain!" many cried. "We have enough rations for the return trip. A new fleet can be assembled and then the search for *el paso* can resume!"

Magallanes pretended not to have heard. "I have named this harbor in honor of San Julián, whose day this is. As well you know, winters are prolonged in extreme latitudes. Therefore we will wait out the rest of winter here, provide our ships with needed repairs, and when the weather improves in a few weeks we will move on."

"You are afraid," yelled Cartagena. He had been released from his shackles to assemble with all ships' companies. It had been many months since I had seen him. Now I tasted my hatred again, remembering how he had used me, how he had been willing to let me die.

Two marines flanked Cartagena on either side, but they could do nothing to keep him silent, and his voice rang through the vast wasteland. "You fear to return to the king with nothing to show. No riches, no passage to the west. You are obsessed with your search for *el paso*. On the flame of your ambition you will crucify us all!"

The captain-general addressed the assembly as if, again, he had not heard. "I have received a report of game in the uplands— much game, hundreds, perhaps thousands, of beasts and fowl. Men, I promise you, we will not hunger. The sea teems with fish and shellfish. And as you can see, there is springwater and fire- wood and materials for building shelter. I assure you the shelters will be warmer than the ships, for we can relax before the fires and sup with bread and wine after our chores have been completed. Winter is almost over and—"

"No!" A sailor screamed. "You are a madman! Cartagena is right! You will kill us all! I demand you take us back to Spain!"

Magallanes whirled, his arm outstretched, his finger pointed. I saw the veins in his neck bulge as he roared, "*¡Sed Preso!*"

A stunned silence followed in which no one dared speak. The wind howled between us, shouting in every ear . . . *¡Sed Preso!* . . . *¡Sed Preso!* . . .

The marines grabbed the sailor, who now looked about him in panic. He struggled, crying, "Help me! Someone, please! Do not suffer this fool to lead us any longer! Why do you just stand there? Why do you not help me? You are cowards, all of you! Cowards—" There was a strange smack. The sound of wood against bone. The sailor's knees buckled and he melted to the rocks.

Magallanes's voice was calm and untroubled once again. "As I have said, winter will not last long, and when it ends, we shall find the passage to the South Seas, where it will only be a short distance, a few weeks at most, before we shall arrive at the Spice Islands." He limped over to stand before Cartagena.

The Castilian drew himself up and towered over the captain-general.

"I would rather die than return to Spain empty-handed," said Magallanes. "The king has entrusted me with this enterprise, and I am honor-bound to succeed. Did not the Vikings sail to Iceland, surviving treacherous fogs and seas of ice? If I must, I will sail until my ships are encased in ice and cannot move." His voice now boomed off the cliffs. "I have heard that Castilians are famed for their pride and courage. Would you now tremble in a brisk wind, a few snowflakes, scurrying back to Spain like a child gone too long from home?"

Although Cartagena's face twisted with fury, he dared not move. For while the captain-general talked, Espinosa had positioned himself beside Magallanes. Even in the waning light Espinosa's sword gleamed. Now Cartagena looked away from Magallanes, furious, saying nothing.

With that, it was decided. For the rest of the day I stumbled around in an aimless way, desperately cold, longing to return to Spain. A horrifying thought kept running through my mind. I tried to shake it, ashamed, but could not. It penetrated like a rotten stench. Perhaps, I thought, Magallanes *is* insane. Perhaps we follow the whims of a madman. Perhaps he will search for *el paso* until there are none left to search but himself, alone aboard the *Trinidad,* the rest of us long dead. Perhaps Rodrigo is right and I am a fool for believing in Magallanes. . . .

The following day was Easter Sunday, and all hands were ordered ashore for Mass.

At first it was only a few whispers. Then, spreading over the company like liquid fire, whispers burned our ears from every direction. "They are missing," whispered Rodrigo. "The two Spanish captains are missing."

"To not attend Mass is a grave offense," whispered someone else.

"Not only that, but all captains, pilots, and officers are invited afterward to a feast aboard the *Trinidad.*"

"To not attend the feast is an insult."

"Likely they plot mutiny."

"Or murder."

"The captain-general pretends he does not notice."

"No doubt he is burning with fury."

Rodrigo whispered, "I have heard a terrible thing. Someone told me that Magallanes swore to the king of Portugal that he would destroy the fleet and maroon all survivors. Perhaps that is what he intends to do in this godforsaken place."

"But why would Magallanes do such a thing?" It made no sense. Nothing made sense anymore.

"It is what everyone says. Can so many men be wrong? Tell me, Mateo, since you are so smart, why does Magallanes not return to Spain? It is the captain-general's pride. Either Magallanes will kill us all for the sake of his ambition, or he will leave us here to rot. Either way, we are doomed."

I awoke on the second day of April to a drizzle of rain. The day was as gray as my mood. Espinosa again asked Rodrigo and me to come with him to fetch wood and water from shore.

Soon we rowed the skiff through quiet waters and a thick mist toward the *San Antonio* to pick up four men who were to join us for the shore party. While we rowed, Espinosa whispered, "Rodrigo, you do not look well this morning. Perhaps it is something you ate?"

Rodrigo shook his head.

I frowned. I had not noticed that Rodrigo looked unwell.

Espinosa paused, then said quietly, "Perhaps then it is something you heard?"

Rodrigo looked up in surprise but said nothing.

"Ah, by your silence you confirm I am right. You are a very proud man, young Rodrigo, and do not think I have not noticed your faithful service as my cabin boy."

A glimmer of a smile appeared on Rodrigo's face. He sat straighter and rowed harder so I was forced to match his pace.

Espinosa continued, "Like I said, you are proud. Too proud. Such a shame, this pride of Castile. So often a sickness in itself."

"A sickness? You call my pride a sickness?" Rodrigo squinted and spat over the side of the skiff.

"Let us suppose a man in Castile is murdered. His brothers, his father, or his sons avenge his death, am I right?"

102

Rodrigo puffed out his chest. "Of course, otherwise the family is dishonored."

"Or if their sister is violated, again they seek revenge."

"Of course."

"Likewise would I," said Espinosa, his face carved of granite in the stark morning light. "But what if someone throws mud upon a man's cloak? Again he kills because his pride is wounded."

"It is so, else there is great dishonor."

"And if a man's family is poor, he must act rich so others think well of him."

"Of course, it is the way of Castile."

"Ah. But I will tell you something I have learned in my years of being a soldier. Honor based only on the opinions of others is poisoned honor. Empty honor. It is no more than false pride and vainglory. Why should a man care if his cloak be muddy? Why should a man impoverish his family just to convince others he is not poor? Throughout Castile, poor men sit idle because they are stiff with pride. They desire others to believe they are noblemen and unworthy of labor with their hands."

I remembered my father's words. *We are not beggars,* he would say. *We are not poor.* But we *were* poor. We had always been poor. I hung my head with shame, wishing I could plug my ears.

Espinosa continued, "Yet true honor is not purchased, but born, and it cares not what others may think. You live your life according to what you know is right. Only that kind of honor is worth seeking and keeping. It is honor within yourself. Do you understand?"

I glanced sidelong at Rodrigo as he blinked with confusion. I wondered. True honor? Honor within yourself? I had a vague understanding, as if I tried to peer through layers of mist to what lay beyond.

"That kind of honor resides in Magallanes," said Espinosa. "He is courageous despite the murmurings of his crew, and with or without their approval he will attempt the impossible. Think on it, Rodrigo, my friend. You have a fierce courage like Magallanes's. Fierce courage others can only dream of. Do not waste it on false pride and false honor. Over the next few days, the next few hours perhaps, I will need honorable men. Are you someone whom I can trust?"

I saw Rodrigo swallow hard. He glanced at me and I knew what he was thinking. Espinosa was loyal to Magallanes. And he was asking Rodrigo to also be loyal. "I—I don't know," said Rodrigo, and his shoulders slumped.

I almost blurted out, "I will be loyal. I am a man of honor. True honor." But Espinosa was not looking at me, and by then our skiff bumped against the hull of the *San Antonio*. The four men we were to meet were nowhere to be seen.

Then a voice said softly from above, "Hark! Who goes there?"

"It is I, Espinosa, master-at-arms."

"Praise God it is you. We thought you would never come."

"Why? What is wrong?"

"Be forewarned. Quesada and his armed men overwhelmed the *San Antonio* last night while we slept. Our captain is below deck in chains. Quesada stabbed our ship's master many times and he now lies dying. Please get help. And hurry. I can say no more. Someone has heard me. I think they come."

"Row to all the ships," Magallanes ordered as soon as Espinosa told him the news. "Ask them their allegiance. We must know who is mutinous and who has remained loyal."

Again we were in the skiff.

Now in a loud voice, Quesada declared from the *San Antonio* that he was captain of the ship and that he owed his allegiance to none but the king. When we rowed to the *Victoria,* Mendoza said the same. And we were not surprised to find Cartagena, freed from his imprisonment, strutting about the *Concepción*'s deck and ordering the men to prepare for warfare.

When we pulled alongside the *Santiago,* Captain Serrano seemed baffled, as if he knew nothing of the mutiny. For when we asked him to whom he owed his allegiance, he responded in a puzzled voice that he owed his allegiance to Magallanes. I was relieved. Serrano had not been named in the letter. Until this moment, I did not know where his loyalties lay. As we rowed back to the *Trinidad,* Serrano's *Santiago* pulled up anchor and followed, aligning itself with the flagship.

It was two against three.

That afternoon, we stared across the mists at the other three ships, their masts thrusting out of the fog like swords. When would they make their move? Would they kill us all? Blow us into the waters with the *San Antonio*'s superior firepower?

A longboat appeared out of the mist. A sailor said he had a message for Magallanes from the three captains. The longboat's crew of eight was invited aboard. They licked their lips and peered around nervously. I knew they feared ambush. Their leader held out the message for the captain-general and, once delivered, stepped back quickly.

Magallanes skimmed the message. He turned to Espinosa. "It is a list of grievances. They say they have suffered much and are sorry to have taken three ships. They request that in the future I obey the king's orders and discuss all matters concerning the fleet with them and consult them regarding my exact course. If I do so, they will acknowledge my leadership and kiss my feet and hands."

Magallanes smiled and handed the message back to the leader. "Tell your captains I would be happy to discuss such arrangements aboard my ship. Please give them my assurances that I will hear them out and do what is right. Espinosa, have the apprentice seaman prepare a feast. I will treat my guests with the honor they deserve."

A feast! Honor! I felt my lip curl with disdain. What did they know of honor? True honor? They have done nothing but deceive and betray.

After Magallanes finished speaking, the leader bowed. Soon the longboat disappeared from sight. It was already growing dark though it was early afternoon.

One hour later, the longboat returned. The leader bowed again before Magallanes. "Sir, they say they dare not board your ship for fear of mistreatment. Instead, they request your presence aboard the *San Antonio,* where they promise to do as you command."

Magallanes regarded the leader. "I must have a moment to consider their request. It—it is not easy to command so many." The captain-general sighed and passed a weary hand over his forehead. Finally he said, "My friend, the seaman has prepared a sumptuous feast and already my stomach growls. Perhaps you and your men are also hungry. It would be a shame to allow such food to go to waste. So come. Rest and sup with me in my cabin, and when we are finished, I will give my reply."

The men of the longboat smiled. They, like us, smelled meat roasting, and I envied their good fortune.

When they had gone into the captain-general's cabin, Espinosa approached me. "Come. I need your help." Again I boarded the skiff, this time without Rodrigo. Espinosa wore a hooded cloak. I saw the flash of steel before he pulled his cloak about him. I wanted to ask him where we were going and why, but the look on his face told me to ask no questions.

In a silence as thick as the newly fallen night, fifteen heavily armed marines slipped into the *San Antonio*'s longboat, moored alongside us. On Espinosa's signal I began to row the skiff into the darkness, leaving the longboat behind.

I strained against the ebb tide and, as ordered, pulled alongside the *Victoria* and tied the skiff. Mendoza peered over the gunwale. He was fully armored except for his helmet. "Who goes there?"

"It is I, Espinosa, master-at-arms."

"What do you want?"

"I must deliver a message to you."

Mendoza blinked nervously and ran his stubby fingers over his goatee. Jeweled rings flashed in the lantern light. "Give me the message."

"I have my orders. I am to deliver the message privately."

Scanning our skiff, Mendoza said, "I am sorry, but I cannot permit anyone to come aboard."

Espinosa laughed, his voice filled with scorn. "The proud Mendoza is frightened of an unarmed messenger? Of a cabin boy? What do you fear, Mendoza? That one and a half men will over-power your ship?"

Even as my ears stung with insult, Mendoza hesitated and then motioned Espinosa aboard. He frowned but made no objection when Espinosa signaled me to follow.

As Espinosa grasped the gangway ladder to climb aboard, he whispered "Stay with me" before disappearing up and over the bulwarks. By the time I climbed aboard, my mind racing, my heart galloping, Mendoza was already escorting Espinosa into his cabin. I hurried to catch up.

"Come in, Mateo, and close the door behind you," said Espinosa.

In the candlelight, I saw Mendoza frown. "I thought you were supposed to give me the message privately."

Instead of replying, Espinosa drew out his message and handed it to Mendoza.

As Mendoza unfolded the paper and began to read, rubbing his beard with jeweled fingers, Espinosa glanced at me out of the corner of his eye. In that instant I knew it to be a trap. I swallowed hard, thinking furiously, I am unarmed. What am I to do? And what if the trap fails? Suddenly I felt very much half a man.

It seemed forever before Mendoza finished reading. Then to my surprise, he smiled, his teeth glinting in the candlelight. "The captain-general humbly begs me to surrender," he said, as if it were a great joke. And he began to laugh. First it was a suppressed chuckle, then a deeper laugh from his chest. Finally, he threw back his head and roared with laughter, his scorn bouncing off the cabin walls and thundering in my ears.

It was then that Espinosa struck.

While Mendoza roared with laughter, Espinosa reached out, grabbed the man's hair, yanked his head savagely back, and buried his knife to the hilt in Mendoza's neck. A startled look popped into Mendoza's eyes. A gurgling. The hairs on the back of my neck stood on end as the man sank to the cabin floor with a creak of armor. A trickle of blood seeped down his neck and vanished under his armor. In the candlelight it looked black.

"You killed him," I said stupidly.

The master-at-arms removed his knife from Mendoza's throat and wiped it clean on his cloak. "Signal the men in the longboat. They are waiting on the starboard side."

"We—we were a diversion," I stammered, trying to understand. "So the longboat could approach in secret."

Espinosa gave me a hard look. "Do what I've asked, Mateo. Go."

Glad to escape the stench of death and my own stupidity, I ran to the starboard side and peered over the gunwale. Out of the darkness, fifteen faces peered up at me. "It is time," I said.

It did not take long. The men of the *Victoria* surrendered once they saw their captain dead and their ship swarming with marines. Together with Espinosa, I raised the flag of Magallanes on the mainmast. "Long live the king and death to traitors!" we cried.

My heart sang with victory; my blood rushed with joy. And in that moment I happily forgave Espinosa his insult, knowing it had been part of a plan—a grand trap he had trusted me with.

We drew up anchor and drifted until the *Victoria* was alongside the *Trinidad*. Along with the *Santiago*, the three ships now guarded the harbor entrance. The tide had turned. The *San Antonio* and *Concepción* were trapped.

I returned with Espinosa to the *Trinidad*.

Later that night I fell into a numb sleep, dreamless, when suddenly, beside me, someone shook Rodrigo awake. It was Espinosa. "Rodrigo. Now is the time."

Rodrigo sat up, his eyes as wide as I had ever seen them.

"Row the skiff to the *San Antonio* and pretend to be a mutineer. Pretend you despise the captain-general and wish to come aboard and join their cause. They will believe you because your hatred of the Portuguese is well known."

Rodrigo said nothing and Espinosa continued, "Wait for the ebb tide, and then when no one is watching, I want you to disable two of their three anchors. That should be enough for the *San Antonio* to drift toward us. We will take care of the rest. Now go."

Like that, he was gone.

I watched as Rodrigo approached the *San Antonio*. Whatever he said was convincing, for no sooner had the skiff touched the hull of the giant vessel than he clambered aboard. Now we waited. I did not sleep again. I stood alone, wondering why Espinosa had trusted Rodrigo with such a mission. Did he not know Rodrigo despised Magallanes?

Throughout the night I stared into the darkness, willing myself to see what was happening. Perhaps Rodrigo was welcomed by the mutineers—heartily clapped on the back for fooling Espinosa, a sword lent to his eager hands. Perhaps, like the others, he waited for daylight and the order to slip past us—cannon blazing—for Spain. Why is it everyone I care about is taken from me? I wondered, my chest tight.

At the first faint light of dawn, I still stood at the bulwarks. The *San Antonio* looked like a ghost, and my heart sank. She had not moved. I don't remember when Espinosa came to stand beside me, but as the sky grew pale, there he was.

And then it happened.

The *San Antonio* began to drift. Slowly at first, then picking up speed.

Espinosa slammed his fist against the gunwale. "He did it! He did it! I knew he would come through!" He turned and ran through the ship. "All hands! All hands! Prepare for battle! Prepare to grapple and board!"

April 3–May 28, 1520

As the *San Antonio* approached, her decks spilled with crew. They ran into each other, confused, dazed with commotion. Captain Quesada, clad in full armor and armed with a lance and shield, strode across the decks, barking orders.

The *Trinidad* shook as she fired a broadside that slammed into the *San Antonio*'s hull. Wood splinters flew and the air quickly filled with smoke.

Grappling hooks soared, snagging the rigging. I pulled on the lines to bring the big ship in close. Armed marines leaped from the *Trinidad* onto the decks of the *San Antonio*. "For whom do you stand?" they cried, brandishing their swords before them. The crew aboard the *San Antonio* raised their hands in surrender. "For King Carlos and Magallanes!"

It was over. As quickly as a knife thrust to the throat.

Quesada and his conspirators were arrested.

A longboat with forty men was dispatched to the *Concepción*. Cartagena surrendered and was imprisoned with Quesada and the other mutineers in the *Trinidad*'s hold.

So. The inexperienced Castilian captains had suffered defeat. It was victory for Magallanes.

But it was a heavy blow. For chained below were two of the remaining four captains and many of the fleet's officers. And the question running through everyone's mind was: Would they all be put to death?

For death was the price of mutiny.

Rodrigo joined me aboard the *Trinidad*. His pale look of yesterday had vanished. When I asked him why he had decided to help Magallanes, Rodrigo spat and said, "I did not help Magallanes. The captain-general is a Portuguese pig."

"Then why did you cut the anchor cables?"

He shrugged. "Maybe I like Espinosa. Maybe someday I will also become a marine."

"What about Cartagena? You like him, too, don't you?"

Suddenly Rodrigo shoved me to the deck. "Do you have to ask so many stupid questions?" he yelled. Then Rodrigo's face turned strange. I was dumbfounded when his lips trembled and his eyes blinked back tears. "They were going to sink the *Trinidad*. I didn't want them to kill you."

I could only stare at him.

Then he punched me in the stomach. I doubled in pain, gasping. "I didn't want them to kill you, because that's my job." He laughed as he fell on me, pounding my ribs.

Birds squawked and circled above us. Again the ships' companies gathered onshore. Again the wind. The cheerless gray of clouds. The never-ending howling as if we were surrounded by demons.

It was the seventh day of April. On this day Quesada was

appointed to die. Four days ago there convened a court-martial. Even the dead Mendoza attended. Propped in his bloodstained armor as if he were yet alive, Mendoza was charged with mutiny alongside his fellow conspirators, forty in all.

All were condemned to death. Mendoza's body was dragged away, beheaded, and quartered. Dismembered parts of his body were suspended from a gibbet, a grisly reminder.

Then the sentence was appealed. It was argued that the ships' companies could not afford such grave loss of life. One of the ships would have to be scuttled. More discussions followed. Punish them harshly, some said, a punishment they will never forget, but do not kill them. Kill only half of them, others argued, and the survivors will dare not rise in rebellion again. Even that loss of life, it was decided, was too costly.

Then Magallanes raised his hand for silence. "The judgment is to be amended," he said. "Only Quesada will be executed. It was he who stabbed the master."

Finally, on this day, we watched in silence as Quesada crossed himself and knelt in the sand, placing his head on the executioner's block. He moved his mane of hair to one side with trembling fingers, exposing his pale neck. Then with a flash of light the ax fell. Quesada's head rolled to the sand, his alabaster hair soaked with blood.

Those guilty of mutiny began the hateful task of careening the ships with their ankles wrapped in chains, all except Cartagena. He was imprisoned in his cabin, for Magallanes dared not allow him access to the ears of so many men, even if those men wore iron shackles. The rest of us began to build barracks and storerooms on a small islet in the bay.

There was one good thing about the mutiny. Minchaca, the marine who had wanted to hurt Aysó, who had then beaten me, was one of the mutineers. Now it was he who was chained. It was he who would suffer. "Who does Magallanes punish now?" I hissed at him one day as he shuffled past me, chains clinking. "Traitor!"

Minchaca stopped and turned. His face looked blank, as if he couldn't remember me. "Dog-Boy?"

I licked my lips, unsure. It had not occurred to me that he wouldn't remember who I was. "Aye," I said.

He said nothing and shuffled on, leaving me standing, reddened with stupidity.

There was an abundance of wood—battered timbers from the ships and a kind of stunted, withered tree that grew on the lower slopes. Immediately we began chopping down trees, sawing, hammering, and drilling. It took us two weeks to build enough barracks and another few days to outfit them with supplies.

Then it snowed and turned bitterly cold. We huddled around the fires in the barracks, the breath of each man clouded with frost, praying for spring to hurry. Cold as it was, the chore of careening the ships remained for those in chains. Come high tide, the convicts floated each ship onto the beach, mooring her fore and aft. Chains clanked as they unloaded cargo and supplies and ballast and shifted the cannon to larboard. As the tide ebbed, the ship rolled on her larboard side, groaning and sighing, weary as an old woman about to sit upon a chair.

During our journey, a mass of sea life had settled upon the ships' hulls, growing with fingers and tentacles that devoured the wood. Barnacles. Stinking seaweed. Such an abundance of colors—greens, reds, yellows, pinks—soft fleshy creatures and those hard as nuts. If unchecked, the marine growth on a ship's hull became an island in itself, thicker than a man was tall, making the ship unwieldy, likely to founder and sink.

The crew of convicts scraped the hulls and replaced battered timbers. They caulked and painted and poured hot tar over both new and old timbers to kill the woodworm and protect the wood. Always the air stank of boiling tar, of smoke from the forge, of tallow, of oakum. The air hissed of bellows, clanged with the banging of iron, buzzed with the hum of saws. The men removed the tattered sails, then scrubbed and mended them. They pumped out the revolting bilges, crawling inside to scour them—a task despised. Then they rolled the ship on her starboard side and began again.

During this period, Cartagena somehow escaped. He went from man to man, desperate, whispering in each ear how Magallanes was mad and how they were all going to die unless something was done, to join with him now, before it was too late. Everyone turned away from him, pretending they hadn't heard, their ears waxed cold. Rodrigo swore it was true, for Cartagena had whispered in his ear, too. Rodrigo told me, "But to join with him now would be suicide."

Cartagena then sat in the shadow of the gibbet. I was gathering wood nearby. Mendoza's and Quesada's severed bodies swayed above him, creaking. And while I watched, he placed their stiffened hands on his cheeks and promised to fulfill their vow. Then he wept. It sounded like paper rubbed together—dry and parched.

It was there by the gibbet that he was arrested. Four marines marched toward him, weapons drawn, their breastplates as gray as the clouds. He did not resist, instead going limp, his boots scraping over the pebbles of the beach as the marines dragged him away. Standing with my load of wood, I searched my heart for my hatred, surprised to find only pity.

The next day another court-martial was held. Into the roaring wind and stinging sleet, and before all the ships' companies, the sentence was announced. Cartagena was to be left behind when the fleet set sail. *Marooned.*

With that lonely word whispering in our ears, we were dismissed. As we walked away, Rodrigo said, "Pah! The captain-general's backbone is limp as a rag. Even now he cannot bring himself to slay the son of a bishop."

I said nothing, wiping the sleet from my eyes. The wind swirled around me, and I pulled my coat close. My teeth ached with cold. The very cliffs howled in torment, singing ghostly songs that promised naught but death. Nothing could be worse than being marooned in this desolate, godforsaken place. Not even Cartagena deserved such a fate.

Hunting, fishing, trapping, and preparing food for storage now consumed our days. Rodrigo and I went with Espinosa to the offshore islands where the black-and-white geese lived. They were easy to kill. A swift blow over the head brought them down. Back at the barracks, we smoked and salted their meat, storing it in casks. We melted their blubber for lamp oil. We scraped their hides and sewed clothing—boots, hats, coats, even rugs for the barracks floor. But within a week our new clothes began to reek, turning stiff and rotten. We wore them anyway.

On the plains high above the cliffs, we found a strange animal with the neck and body of a camel, the head and ears of a mule, and the tail of a horse. These we killed with crossbows. When I washed the blood and salt from my hands, I drew one into my sketchbook so I would not forget what they looked like. The pelts were even finer than that of the seawolf.

Mussels and crabs grew in the muddy bottoms near the shore. We roasted them and ate them while they were still hot, burning our fingers and throats. Wildfowl were tricky to kill. Rodrigo was expert at bringing them down with a stick thrown through the air. When they fell, stunned, we clubbed them to death.

One day the pimply-faced boy, the master's lover, walked from our islet into the sea. Over the roar of the wind I begged him to return, but he did not look back. While I watched, the waters lapped over his head and he disappeared. I stood there for an hour. My teeth chattering. My heart hollow. Praying for forgiveness. But I felt nothing, heard nothing but the endless, bone-numbing wind.

Not long after, a blizzard pounded us with its fist, furious and raw. No one could go outside, not even the men in chains. Men lay about on their furs, sewing pelts, occasionally stoking the fires, wondering why spring continued to hide her face. After all, it was May.

As I sat upon my bedding, drawing in my sketchbook, the fleet's astrologer said something that caused all to sink into silence, punched in the stomach with despair.

"I believe I know why the weather worsens and the days become shorter." I stopped to stare for his voice was grave. "Just as the stars are different in the Northern Hemisphere, so also are the seasons. When it is winter in the Northern Hemisphere, it is summer here. When it is winter here, it is summer there."

"What are you saying?" someone cried.

"Today is the twenty-eighth day of May. If we were in Spain, summer would soon begin with the solstice in June. But here in the Southern Hemisphere, June heralds the start of winter. That is why the days have become shorter."

A profound sense of nothingness pierced me. It cannot be. Beneath my furs, where none could hear me, I wept. Shuddering sobs, like none I had wept before.

Winter.

It had just begun.

XV

May 28–August 24, 1520

". . . and through the wind and waves he rowed. Rowing, rowing, until his muscles screamed and he overtook the junk. He boarded it and single-handedly defeated fifty of the Chinese—"

"You are making this up," interrupted Rodrigo. "No man could defeat fifty men by himself."

"I swear it upon my soul," said Gutiérrez, a cabin boy younger than I. "No doubt the captain-general wore full armor."

"If he wore full armor, then he could not have rowed like a madman through such weather."

"May the earth swallow me whole if this be a lie." Gutiérrez paused, as if waiting to see if he spoke the truth. "Then, after all the Chinese lay dead, he rescued his friends from their prison below deck and from then on they sailed the junk."

Rodrigo spat. "Tales."

Gutiérrez turned to me. "You believe me, don't you, Mateo?"

When I started to answer, Espinosa spoke from behind me. I had not even known he was there. "Your tale is a little stretched, but it makes for fine listening." He moved to sit beside me on my bedding. "The captain-general is a brave and good man. He has done many miraculous things in his life. There was the time when, as a young officer, he was shipwrecked with the ship's company on an atoll. They had only a few small boats, skiffs probably, but certainly not enough room for everyone."

"Let me guess," said Rodrigo with a wicked smile. "Magallanes swam back home with everyone clinging to his back. In full armor, no less."

Instead of laughing, Espinosa's face hardened, and he said, "You would do well to admire him, Rodrigo, for he has many fine traits that in you I find lacking." Rodrigo clapped his mouth shut and Espinosa continued, "The ship's officers planned to set off in the skiffs, promising to send a party back to rescue the common crew. But the crew protested, saying the ship's officers meant to abandon them."

"Did they?" I asked.

"They had planned on it. What did the officers care about the crew? After all, the officers were aristocrats, sons of nobles, and the crew naught but commoners. The scene grew ugly, and when it seemed certain blood would flow, Magallanes stepped forward and offered to stay behind with the crew while the rest of the officers fetched help."

"And what happened?"

"The crew loved him for it, and the officers left without bloodshed. For three weeks Magallanes and the crew suffered under the scorching sun with few provisions."

"I take it they were rescued," said Rodrigo, "else Magallanes would not be here."

"Yes, they were rescued. His selfless act was talked about for many months."

"Just as how he is killing us now will be talked about for many years?" retorted Rodrigo. "Magallanes has marooned us here to die. We have only rotten goose meat and biscuit to eat. Plus he has sent the *Santiago* on a fool's mission, looking for a passage that does not exist. They have been gone for weeks. They are probably shipwrecked, and this time His Holiness is not there to save them. Maybe he will send each ship out, one by one, until we are all dead."

Espinosa fixed his gaze on Rodrigo. "Why do you hate him so, my friend?"

Rodrigo shrugged.

Espinosa was silent a long time before saying, "It is time to let your hatred go. It is time to stop punishing him for merely being Portuguese. Magallanes has been commissioned with an impossible task—to establish a westward route to the Spice Islands—a mission few in this world would dare attempt, much less accomplish. Give him room to succeed, my friend, and perhaps he shall surprise you."

Each day we watched from our islet for the *Santiago*.

Each day we saw nothing but the endless stretch of gray sea.

On the third day of June, I turned fifteen years old. It has been one year, I thought, since my parents died, since I left Ávila, since I slept in the ditch by the river of mud. I have been through much. I brushed my fingers over my sparse whiskers, thinking, I am a man.

Shortly after midday, we saw a strange and wonderful sight. Never in all the time since we had been in Port San Julián had we seen another human being. In fact, not since the cannibals. Yet on this day, we saw a native. He was a giant, huge and well formed. When he saw us standing before the barracks, he danced on the shore of the mainland, twirling and leaping.

Magallanes ordered a seaman ashore in a skiff to invite the giant to our islet. At first the giant would not come, crossing his arms and planting his feet. Then the seaman did a hilarious thing. He pranced around the giant, dancing the same ridiculous dance. It worked. The giant smiled and climbed into the skiff.

When he came to the islet, we gathered about him, astonished at his great height. He was at least ten palms high and even the tallest Castilian among us did not reach above his neck. Except for yellow encircling his eyes, his entire face was painted red, with black heart-shaped emblems on his cheeks. He carried bow and arrows, the string of the bow made from animal gut and the arrows like ours except they had a stone point instead of iron. He wore the skins of the same animals we had found on the upper plains, only his clothing was well stitched and he placed them around his feet as well, leaving gigantic footprints wherever he stepped.

We quickly fetched him gifts from our trade stores. He glanced at himself in a mirror and shrieked, falling backward. When he recovered, we gave him mirrors and bells, combs and rosary beads. We offered him food and he devoured an amount that would have fed five men, maybe ten. It was astounding. Afterward, we rowed the giant back to the mainland.

That evening Magallanes ordered full rations of wine. For the first time in weeks I played my guitar. The men drummed rhythms, sang songs, laughed, and drank much wine.

The native did not return the next day, nor the next. Our vigil for the *Santiago* continued, only now we also watched the mainland for signs of natives.

By mid-June, the world outside turned a ghostly white, burying the ships under ice and snow. Our mood blackened. We sickened of so much meat. We tired of our barracks, now filthy with the stink of many men living together. We hated the wind that constantly howled, night and day, seeping through the cracks of the barracks to mock the fires. One of our shipmates was sick, the stench surrounding his bedding so nauseating we grew irritable to smell it and argued whose turn it was to change his furs.

One day when I told Rodrigo it was his turn, he pounded the wall of the barrack with his fist. "I cannot stand this! I must get out of here or I will go crazy." Then he turned to me and, indeed, he looked crazy. His hair stood on end, messy and unshorn. Stubble covered his face. He stared at me, his eyes wide and frantic, until I could see the whites all around them. I could smell his breath, hot and foul. "Mateo. I will pay you a ducat to change his bedding for me."

"You do not have a ducat any more than I do."

"I swear to you, as soon as I am wealthy, I shall pay you."

"But I will be wealthy, too. What will one little ducat matter to me?"

"A thousand ducats then."

"You will never have so much money."

"I promise you, one day I shall be the wealthiest man in Spain."

"Wealthier than the king?"

"The second wealthiest then. You can be my financial advisor."

"Then, as your financial advisor, I advise you to save your money and change the bedding yourself."

"Mateo, please."

"No."

"Mateo, please. I beg of you. If not for money, then for my sake." And he stared at me with those crazy eyes.

I sighed and rolled my eyes. But I did what he asked, cursing with disgust until the task was done. "You owe me," I said later.

He nodded and ran his hand through his hair. "I won't forget, my friend. God help me, I hate this place."

It was like that. These conversations. Crazy and desperate, as if this were a nightmare from which we couldn't awaken. I hated this place, too. But now I wondered if Rodrigo was losing his mind.

Rodrigo had been right about one thing. The *Santiago* had indeed been shipwrecked. This we discovered when the survivors returned and told their tale.

"So now we are four ships instead of five," complained Rodrigo. "We will be many men crammed together—if we ever leave this accursed place, that is. Do you realize, Mateo, that when we leave we will continue southward? There is no end. There is no mercy."

"Be quiet, Rodrigo. You should be happy the *Santiago*'s men are safe."

"We are none of us safe."

"Stop it, Rodrigo. Think about other things. Think about Spain and the happy day we return."

"That's just it, Mateo." He looked me full in the face.

"What do you mean?"

"Perhaps no one will live to see Spain again. Not even you."

I blinked at him stupidly. "Don't say that. You curse us with such thoughts. Of course we will return to Spain. All of us." But, for some reason, my words sounded hollow, and I was forced to look away.

In celebration of the return of the *Santiago*'s crew, Magallanes ordered wine for everyone. Again I brought out my guitar. Then Magallanes ordered the chains struck forever from the mutineers, provided they remained loyal. "They have suffered enough," he proclaimed.

Cartagena, moved to the barracks when the weather turned too bitter aboard ship, said nothing as they struck the chains from his ankles. He seemed but a shadow of the proud man I had first seen aboard the *San Antonio*, alone and silent, as if he were already marooned. It is enough, I thought. Enough that he should suffer so. We have all suffered. Let it end.

I wanted to tell him I was sorry. I wanted to tell him that he was no longer my enemy, that I no longer hated him. Several times I approached him where he sat staring into the fire. But my tongue cleaved to the roof of my mouth and instead I walked away.

One day there was a terrible fistfight. It exploded from the area around the fire when someone wouldn't make room for someone else. Fists flew and curses erupted. I saw a smear of blood, a pockmarked face, and knew one of the men was Segrado. Espinosa broke up the fight, forcing the men apart. Segrado's chest heaved, and he had the look of murder in his eyes. Then, to the utter amazement of all, including Segrado, he burst into tears—deep, wracking, silent sobs. Espinosa let him go when he thrust his way out of the barracks and into the cold. When the door closed behind him, there was an embarrassed silence.

Since leaving Brazil, Segrado had never bothered me again, not even to look at me. It was a relief, but that was many months ago. To see him reduced to tears shook even me. Later that evening I was sitting by one of the fires eating my supper when Segrado stumbled into the circle beside me to warm his hands. He smelled of cold, and his body trembled beneath his clothes. Suddenly, I handed him my plate. "It's hot," I said.

He gaped at me, his nose red and dripping, his beard crusted with ice. Then, finally, he grunted, crouched, and began shoveling food into his mouth.

On my other side, Rodrigo hissed in my ear, "If you weren't hungry, why didn't you give it to me? Why did you do so foolish a thing?"

I shrugged, remembering the pimply-faced boy who walked into the sea and the proud Castilian captain sentenced to die.

As the days passed, we continued to watch for natives. It gave us something to do besides fight each other. We decided to capture a few of them, to take them to Spain as a gift for the king. Six days after the return of the *Santiago*'s crew, two giants appeared onshore. They were good specimens, each painted with a different design. This time a crew of twelve men, including Magallanes, was dispatched in a longboat toward the mainland to greet the natives. I watched from the islet, as did all the others. I thought perhaps the natives would suspect something was wrong, but they smiled and danced when the longboat touched shore.

Magallanes ordered the natives be loaded with gifts. Even from the islet, I saw their delight. Then Magallanes gave each of them a set of iron shackles. They seemed pleased and sought to hold the iron shackles but could not because their arms over-

127

flowed with gifts. Magallanes knelt before them and placed the shackles about their ankles, indicating that in this way they could carry them and their gifts as well. At first they were happy, but when they tried to walk, they realized they had been fooled. They cast their gifts to the ground and bellowed like the bulls of Spain.

There were congratulations among everyone. We had done it. We had easily captured two natives. They were brought to the islet and housed in the barracks. Once they saw we meant no harm, though still seeming sad, they stopped their bellowing.

They quickly adapted to life in the barracks. Each of them could eat a basket of biscuit and drink half a bucket of water in one gulp. Never had we seen such appetites. We also watched in fascinated horror when they ate rats, not bothering to skin them first.

Now we dared not go to the mainland except in armed parties of forty men or more, for we were constantly pestered by scores of angry natives. So although winter yet continued, it was agreed: it was time to move camp.

On a misty day in August, as a light snow drifted from the sky, Espinosa and I marooned Cartagena and his two dogs on an islet. The islet was nothing more than a pile of boulders jutting from the harbor waters, barren, white with snow. There we left him a supply of biscuit and wine.

Cartagena brushed the snow off a rock, sat down, and arranged his cloak around him. He said nothing, instead staring out across the vast waters as if he could see through the mists all the way to Spain.

I wanted to tell him I did not wish to see him left behind. That no one deserved such a fate. "Cartagena, I—I—"

128

He held up his hand to stop me, still not looking at me, staring only across the ocean. "Please, say nothing."

"But I—I . . ." My voice trailed away. How stupid I sounded.

The dogs whined. One of them licked Cartagena's hand, and steam rose from the dog's breath.

And then, before I could stop myself, I blurted, "If you would promise upon your life not to mutiny again, maybe Magallanes would reconsider. He has never wished you ill. Only that you would stop trying to—"

At this, Cartagena threw back his head and laughed. It was a shrill laughter, a needle in the ear. It pierced my bones and shattered my words. On and on he laughed. Tears slid down his cheeks. The dogs cocked their heads. Finally, the laughter faded, and gasping for breath, Cartagena looked at me. A chill spread through my spine like a disease, for in his eyes I saw death.

"Is life really so simple for you, Mateo?" Still breathing hard, Cartagena studied me. "Ah, yes, I see that it is. Do you know that sometimes I envy you? With nothing to think about except eating, sleeping, and breathing? Seems funny, does it not? That I would envy you?"

I did not answer.

"Will you trade places with me now?" He stared at me, his eyes deadened in their sockets. "I will be Mateo, and you, the young, dashing captain? No?" He returned his gaze toward the sea. "Pity."

A gust of wind rippled the water. Snow swirled at our feet like white dust. Nearby a seabird floated in the air, caught in a current of wind, motionless. A hand pressed my shoulder. It was Espinosa. "Come," he said, pulling me gently away.

"Wait," I said, facing Cartagena for what would be the last time. "Is that all? You will not even try?"

He did not look at me again. "Tell my mother not to grieve," he said finally. "Tell my father I'm sorry I failed him. That is all."

I stumbled into the boat. As we rowed away, my heart pinched and heavy, I knew. As long as Cartagena had breath within him, strength to raise a dagger even, he would forever rise against the captain-general. It was a bitter understanding.

The weather detained us for another thirteen days, but finally, on the twenty-fourth day of August, in the year of our Lord 1520, the fleet sailed from Port San Julián, leaving Cartagena behind.

XVI

August 24–November 28, 1520

We wintered for two more months in the harbor where the *Santiago* was lost. In mid-October the weather improved enough to strike winter camp. It was what we had waited for, and we bustled about like ants, bumping into one another in our rush to leave. For myself, I felt a lightness in my heart I had not felt for many months. It was the warmer weather, yes, but also a longing to quit this whole land, to forget that the soil seeped with blood and betrayal.

We sailed south in search of *el paso*.

On the twenty-first day of October, we entered a bay where the water was the color of a light blue gemstone and the beaches gleamed of white sand. When the mists parted, I glimpsed snow-capped mountains stretching far inland. There would be no passage here. The water was too shallow and no passage could cross such mountains.

"A mission of stupidity," whispered Rodrigo when Magallanes ordered the *San Antonio* and *Concepción* to explore the bay. Even from where I stood, I saw the dark looks cast toward the captain-general.

As the two ships sailed deep into the bay, the sky suddenly blackened. The wind whipped the caps from our heads, and the heavens opened with a violent storm. Those of us aboard the *Trinidad* and *Victoria* watched in horror as the *San Antonio* and *Concepción* careened toward a gigantic rock that jutted over both land and water.

They vanished in a confusion of spray and waves.

Monstrous waves towered over us, crashing over the decks. Men were swept overboard. Thunder roared in our ears and lightning rattled our teeth. The sea swept through the *Trinidad*'s hatches, poured through her gun ports. We manned the pumps, desperate, praying. To do anything else was death. Through the spray and blinding wind and flashes of lightning I glimpsed the *Victoria,* dismasted.

Two days later, when finally the storm ended, the *Trinidad* and *Victoria,* wounded and bleeding, limped their way back into the bay. There were no signs of the other ships. We had surely lost them. The shores were bare. There were no survivors. No wreckage. A chill ran through me as I remembered the words of Rodrigo spoken so long ago, more than a year prior. *If we are lucky, half of us will return. It is the way of the sea.*

We conducted our repairs ashore in silence, speaking only to ask for a tool or to give instructions. No one looked at anyone else. Our grief was too enormous, unspeakable—so many men lost. Had they come this far only to perish? I wondered. To drown in an instant, before they could even make confession, their sins unforgiven? Perhaps Rodrigo had cursed us with such a pronouncement. I slipped behind a tree and prayed the rosary—once, twice, three times. And as I gazed into a sky of lead, cold and distant, I vowed, curse or not, to return to Spain. The sea shall not claim Mateo Macías de Ávila.

After repairs, we continued our search and began to edge past the rock where the ships had disappeared. Perhaps the wreckage lay behind it.

"Smoke!" cried the lookout.

We peered around the rock and, indeed, a thin column of smoke snaked like a scar into the sky. Maybe there were survivors! We sailed farther, and when we passed the rock, we caught our breath in amazement.

Before us, through the snowcapped mountains, lay a deep-water passageway, stretching for many leagues, that had been hidden from sight by the rock. While each of us yet stared, there came the cry "Two sail! Closing fast!" We scrambled up the shrouds to see. There! There in the distance, with every scrap of canvas to their yards, the *Concepción* and *San Antonio* sailed toward us, cannon blasting, flags waving.

"God be praised!" cried our lookout. And, hanging from the shrouds, our voices joined his, each of us grinning and shouting with joy, hailing our shipmates as they approached.

The *San Antonio* hove to alongside the flagship. Her captain stepped aboard and bowed before Magallanes. He was breathing heavily and his eyes danced with an excitement we had not seen for many months. "My captain-general, I have the honor to report the discovery of *el paso*. It is a narrow, deep strait, with a heavy tidal flow, and we penetrated many leagues before turning back." He outlined the route they had taken, the succession of bays, the presence of salt in the water. "It is *el paso,* I tell you. We have found it!"

Magallanes smiled, and we cheered as the gunners fired

salutes. What a glorious day! Not only had we found our lost ship-mates, but also the passage!

"*El paso! El paso!*"

"A few short days and we will be in the South Sea!"

"Perhaps in no more than a week we shall arrive at the Spice Islands!"

"God be praised that the worst is behind us!"

On the first day into the strait, excitement surged through the crew of the *Trinidad*. Since the end of March we had lived in the gut of winter. Now it was time to sail to warmer seas, to paradise. Stories of Magallanes circled the deck—stories of his past hero-ism, stories of honor, of courage. Gutiérrez never tired of the telling, and Magallanes grew like a god in the eyes of the crew, even, I believe, in the eyes of Rodrigo. "Through this man's mad-ness," he said, "I will become rich. It was a good day I signed for this voyage."

I brought out my guitar. Though the weather was brisk, it was springtime in the south. In honor of the season I sang a song of maidens, of young love. I composed another song about Aysó. As I sang, the clouds parted, the sun shone bright, and the breeze snatched white clouds of breath from my mouth.

Come nightfall, fires dotted the land to the south. They were far away and silent. The next day we saw what appeared to be a village on an inland hill to the northwest, less than half a league from shore.

I approached Espinosa as he prepared an armed party to inves-tigate. Always before, I had scouted for wood, or food, or water. Never a village. "Let me come with you," I said.

"For what purpose?"

"None," I stammered. "I—I just want to go."

"No." He slid his polished sword into his scabbard, turned, and left me.

Upon sudden inspiration, I ran after him. "Espinosa, wait. Our court-appointed artist was washed overboard in the last storm, and now there is no one to draw pictures of our voyage." I puffed out my chest and held my head high. "Therefore, in addition to my regular duties, I will draw sketches of what I see, including the village. It will be official. I am the best there is. You have no choice."

He regarded me. "Such fine words, Mateo. Let's hope you live up to them. Fetch your things, for we leave now."

The men from the ships watched as we picked our way past bleached bones, past the rotting carcass of a great whale whose ribs jutted upward, exploding with stink and hundreds of screaming seabirds. Out of the corner of my eye I saw cabin boys lining the rails. I pretended not to notice that they gaped at me as I marched with the marines. I threw back my shoulders and held my head high, thinking, I am now the official artist of the voyage. If all goes well, I will someday be famous. Invited to court to show the king the miraculous things I have seen and done. I will be given money. And land. All shall clamor for my attention. It is a far cry from a poor shepherd's son.

The forest closed around us as I followed Espinosa and ten heavily armed marines. I heard nothing but the tramp of boots upon the path as we wound through the trees, upward toward the village. As the trees loomed over me, quiet and vast, an odd thing happened. An unsettled feeling began to follow me, as if someone breathed on the back of my neck. I kept glancing behind me but saw no one.

Then I heard it.

A whisper.

. . . *Go away* . . .

Again, no one.

Again, the breath against my neck.

. . . *Go away* . . .

It is a ghost, I thought, my heart hammering wildly. An evil spirit. It wishes me ill and will cast a spell on me if I do not leave. If I do not flee. Now.

Gooseflesh prickled my skin and I resisted the urge to run to the safety of the ships. Instead I coaxed my feet forward. I refused to look backward anymore. I decided I would not give the ghosts the satisfaction of seeing me frightened. Ghosts! Pah! I marched in rhythm, our footsteps as one.

We left the forest of ghosts and marched up the barren hill, our pikes thrust upward into the gray sky. A wind blew, hollow and bleak. When we reached the top, instead of the village we expected, strange platforms circled the hill like a crown. We entered the circle, armed, breathing hard. Where were the people? Except for the wind that swirled over the ground and moaned between the platforms, it was eerily silent.

"Spread out," said Espinosa, his voice unnaturally loud. "See if we can find anything of use to us."

The platforms rose on irregular sticks, ending above my head in a bed of thatch. I settled beside a platform and began to draw. After all, that was my job now, was it not? The sketch was bold and vivid, but even so, it was inaccurate. For how does one draw the wind? The emptiness? The fear on the face of each marine? The whispers against the back of our necks, shouting louder, louder.

. . . *Go away* . . .

Then it happened.

With a heave-ho, one of the marines hoisted another marine atop a platform. The platform swayed and toppled in a clatter of weapons, curses, and sticks. A corpse tumbled from the platform, decapitating upon impact. The skull rolled and bounced onto my legs. Blackened skin stretched over the skull like leather, exposing the teeth in a grin of death. And beneath a headdress of seabirds' feathers, shriveled eyes stared at me.

A mummy.

Horrified, I screamed and kicked the skull. It soared out of the circle and bounced down the hill.

. . . *Go away!* . . .

My blood boiled with terror. Without waiting for anyone, I fled down the hill and along the forest path, hair flying.

. . . *Go away!* . . .

Ghosts swarmed over me. I screamed as I ran, reckless, tripping over stones, leaping over streams and logs, my lungs afire. *God in heaven! Help me!* Finally, I reached the beach of bones and flew into the longboat to hide.

"Mother Mary, have mercy!" I crossed myself again and again.

Seconds later the longboat filled with marines, their faces white as candle wax. I saw many arms making the sign of the cross.

"God save us!"

"Holy Mother of God!"

"Blessed Virgin, save us!"

Only Espinosa took his time coming from the village. The men cursed having to wait for him, and as soon as he entered the longboat, we flew like a bird across the waters, our oars like wings.

"It was a burial ground," Espinosa told Magallanes once we'd boarded the *Trinidad*. "Nothing but thatched mounds that held the bodies of giant natives, their skin not even rotted but stretched and dried atop their bones. It was unholy. Let us leave—and quickly."

The cabin boys gathered around me as we left our anchorage.

"There he is," mocked Rodrigo, grinning. "Mateo, the big bad warrior. Afraid of nothing."

Blood rushed to my face and I shoved him. "Try holding a mummy's head while spirits scream in your ears and tell me you would not run as well!"

"Was she pretty?" Gutiérrez asked.

"Did you get lucky?" asked Rodrigo as he and the other cabin boys collapsed into laughter. I turned away.

That evening, Magallanes called me to his cabin. "Espinosa tells me you wish to be the official artist of the voyage."

I hung my head. "I cannot."

"Tell me why."

Again my face burned. "I left all my drawing supplies at the burial site. All I have is my sketchbook."

"An error I trust will not happen again. Use the supplies of the last artist and draw the burial site from memory. I must have a visual record. If it is good, then you will be the official artist, and the supplies are yours to keep. Do you understand?"

I spent a number of days on the sketch, scanning my mind for details, pleased with the quality of the materials I now had to work with. A fine inkhorn. A velvet-lined box of inks and sharpened goose quills. A pounce pot filled with powder for absorbing excess ink.

During this time, the passageway gradually veered south and

then forked. The ships hove to and the pilots and captains conferred. Then again we sailed forward. The *San Antonio* sailed the left fork while the other three ships sailed the right fork. Already we were many leagues into the strait, farther than the *Concepción* and *San Antonio* had gone before.

As we continued southward, I showed Magallanes my sketch.

For a long time he studied it, his brow wrinkled, saying nothing. Finally he gave it back to me. "What else do you have?"

I retrieved my sketchbook.

He cocked his eyebrow, studying first one sketch, then another. A chronicle of the voyage. "Where did you learn to draw?" he finally asked.

"My mother taught me."

"She must have been a woman of great skill and training, for she has taught you well. The supplies are yours."

Cabin boy, musician, artist—it was much to do, but I did not mind. Someday, I thought, someday I shall be famous, and the extra work now mine will seem as nothing. I am Mateo Macías, official artist of the voyage of Magallanes.

Shortly thereafter we rounded a cape and entered a wide sound that took two days to cross. Sheer cliffs towered above the shores and the currents were treacherous. As we approached the end, it again forked. The southern fork looked not to be the passageway, for it was narrow and great mountains loomed ahead of it. We instead turned to the northwest fork. As we continued to round the cape, the passage stretched northwest for as far as the eye could see.

Magallanes's face sparkled with excitement. "Take the *Concepción* and go back to the rendezvous point to meet the *San*

Antonio," he said to the captain of the *Concepción* once the ships came alongside. "The *Victoria* and I will continue up the strait and search for a suitable anchorage. We must reprovision before we set sail on the South Sea."

The sights were magnificent. Heavily wooded mountains rose to dizzying heights on both sides. Rivers of snow sparkled in the sun, blinding me. Streams emptied into the passage, their banks swollen, their waters swift from the ice melt of spring. After a day's sail, we anchored in a small bay teeming with sardines.

Immediately I left my inks, for there was much work to be done. Besides ship repairs, we snared seabirds and rabbits while netting and smoking thousands of sardines. I was glad there were no ghosts here, no whispers. Still, as I scoured out the water casks and filled them with fresh water from the stream, I could not help glancing over my shoulder. Rodrigo laughed and called me a coward, but I saw him glance, too.

When neither the *Concepción* nor the *San Antonio* returned by the twelfth day of November, Magallanes ordered us to set sail in search of the two vessels. We found the *Concepción* a short distance up the strait, but her captain said he had searched everywhere and could not find the *San Antonio*.

We searched many days for the lost ship. Since she was the largest vessel of the fleet, and therefore considered the most seaworthy, she had been given the bulk of the provisions.

Despite our search, we found nothing.

The *San Antonio* was gone.

It was a terrible loss.

We had no choice but to continue up the passage, past the Bay of Sardines, finally arriving at the western mouth of the strait, where the open waters stretched before us.

At daybreak on the twenty-eighth day of November, we stood out to sea. The first two hours were difficult, for it was the point where the sea met the outgoing tide and the waters whipped themselves into a frenzy. It took all of the captain-general's skill to lead us where the waters were as calm as the day we left Spain.

The midday sun hailed us through the clouds as all ships' companies knelt in prayer. Dressed in dazzling vestments, standing high on the flagship's poop, the padre raised a brass crucifix to the heavens and called upon the grace of Our Lady of Victory. As he led us in a hymn, tears streamed down my face. I could not help it.

The cannon blew a broadside. Seabirds scattered from the yards in a flurry of feathers and shrieks. Standing beside the flag of Castile—beside the lions, the castles—Magallanes cried, "We are about to enter waters where no ship has sailed before. May this sea be always as calm as it is today! In this hope I name it the *Mar Pacifico!*"

XVII

November 28, 1520–January 9, 1521

As the fleet pointed north for warmer waters, we lounged in the shadow of the fo'c'sle. Cabin boys and marines, seamen and barbers. Spaniards, Portuguese, Italians, and French, deciding among ourselves the value of the spices we would soon receive and how to best spend our riches.

"For myself, I shall want a bag of pepper."

"A bag! You do not know how to dream. I shall want ten bags! A hundred!"

"Neither of you will remember pepper once you have tasted nutmeg. I tasted it once in Seville, and let me tell you, nutmeg is the finest spice you will ever smell or eat."

"Ah, but I hear nutmeg cannot preserve meat like pepper."

"Idiots, all of you. I care not what spices taste good or smell divine. Only a fool eats his spices. For me, I shall sell mine. It is the only wise thing to do. I have heard that in the Spice Islands one can purchase a ducat's worth of cloves and sell it in Seville for one hundred ducats."

"We shall all be rich!"

"With my money, I shall buy my wife a house in the city."

"My wife shall have a new dress. No, ten new dresses. And gold earrings so heavy she must rest them on her shoulders. And a pearl necklace. She will look like nobility."

"Pah! To spend money on a woman is foolishness. I will spend my money on me, and if my wife does not like it, she can sail to the Spice Islands and get her own spices."

"I do not have a wife."

"You are lucky. Wives suck the money from a man's pocket until he is destitute and dishonored."

"I have a good wife. She does not spend money. She cooks and cleans and has borne me a son every year for five years."

"You, too, are lucky."

"Yes. Lucky. Juana was with child when I left. If all went well, I have a new son. Perhaps he is one year old today."

One pleasant December day, Magallanes ordered the fleet to turn to the northwest. Dolphins swam alongside the bow, jumping and playing, as light and happy as our mood. We knew the Spice Islands were just beyond the horizon.

Magallanes spent his days pacing the quarterdeck, afterward pouring over the many charts inside his cabin. "Ah, Mateo," he would say as I entered to begin my watch. "Come, see our destiny." With a short finger he stabbed at a squiggle or a blotch upon his nautical charts. I would nod, knowing such things meant continents, or seas, or islands. To me, the charts were meticulous and stunning. Sometimes, when he wasn't looking, I brushed my fingers over the paper, thinking, I am here. Sailing upon a chart.

Then as the stars became visible each twilight, he bade me fetch his nautical instruments, saying, "Follow me." From his cabin and onto the deck I stepped, following the commander, both my arms and my head bursting with importance. He peered at the stars with his instruments, making notations aloud. Any day, I knew, he would pronounce the Spice Islands to be just over the horizon. Perhaps I would be the first to tell my shipmates. *Prepare your sea chests for gold and spices, rubies and silks,* I would say, *for tomorrow we arrive at the Spice Islands. The captain-general has said so.*

Instead of gold and spices, rubies and silks, Magallanes ordered all the cabin boys to boil tar in the cauldrons and coat the rigging, the bulwarks, the lines, and every seam we could see. There are many seams in a ship. We groaned, complaining. It was toilsome work, filled with stink, and hot as hell itself. After four days of drudgery, the *Trinidad* was as black as the day she left Spain. We stowed the cauldrons and sat about, aching, our skin blackened and sticky, dreaming about the day when we could trade our tar brushes for gold.

But the days grew long. Still we searched the western horizon for land. The seabirds that had cluttered our ship abandoned us and flew back to the continent. The dolphins left as well. Now the sea seemed empty. Nothing but sky and sea.

As the decks warmed, becoming a furnace, we grew listless. All chores, all yarns, all singing, all dreams of the future, melted to nothing. I played my guitar, but then my hands would cease their strumming. My voice would trail into vapor and I would find myself staring at the vast sea. Staring . . . thinking nothing . . .

Then the giant native from Port San Julián became ill. He was our only native, for the other had been aboard the *San Antonio*. We had been so certain the giant would survive the journey, for he was stronger than any of us. He laughed as he bent the shafts of our harquebuses while eating enough to feed a horse. But warmer weather made him ill. We baptized him and showed him the cross. He kissed it many times, dying with it pressed to his lips. Now a horde of sharks followed. Their triangular fins sliced through our wake.

One evening when the *Victoria* swung by for her nightly salute, we learned there was a sickness aboard their ship, a sickness that swelled the gums and left fetid breath. On that day one of their men died of this unknown plague. I watched as they cast his body overboard, turning away when the water churned with sudden violence. Perhaps this is it, I thought. Perhaps after all this time, it has found me. I burned the farm to destroy it. I fled Ávila to escape its deadly poisons, yet the pestilence chased me to the very edge of the world.

With the disappearance of the *San Antonio,* we had lost much of our provisions. Rations had been cut in half a week before, and I suffered from hunger. My throat dried and my tongue thickened with thirst. In spite of the captain-general's impressive nautical charts and instruments, I began to wonder if we had passed the last land known to man and sailed instead toward the edge of the earth, where the water dropped off into emptiness. Rodrigo laughed at me, telling me such fancies were old tales, that all knew the earth was round and that if we kept sailing we would someday arrive back in Spain. Yet even he stopped laughing as the days passed and the sea stretched on. Staring . . . thinking nothing . . .

Magallanes's mood became somber. Now when I entered his cabin, he did not seem to know I was there. He hunched over his maps, his forehead creased. When I set food before him and returned an hour later, it was untouched.

Each day, the sun blazed—an enemy, unbearable. My lips blistered and my skin peeled. So hot. So thirsty. Each night the stars appeared numberless, and I saw five brilliant stars in the western sky arranged like a cross. Perhaps God has not abandoned me, I thought.

On one cloudless day, another body slipped from the *Victoria* into the sea. It was Segrado. The water boiled, bubbling with red. I saw his arm here, his leg there, the silvery flash of sharks as they broke the surface of the water, jerking back and forth, fighting over his torso. Then it was over. I crumpled to the deck, sickened, my face in my hands.

The meat turned putrid and glowed in the dark. Fat white maggots writhed in it. The maggots ate not only meat, but leather, ships' timbers, even our woolen clothing. At first I squished them, hating their blind, wriggling bodies, but then as my hunger increased, I ate them. We all did. We had no choice. I turned from Rodrigo so he would not see me gag.

The wine barrels stood empty. Now we had only water to drink, yet even the water became vile. Yellow. Swimming with vermin. It smelled so bad we plugged our noses for our daily cup.

"It is piss," whispered Rodrigo one day as we lined up for our ration.

"Piss?"

"Why do you think it is nasty and yellow? It is because someone drank all the water and then pissed in the barrels."

"Who?"

"How should I know? I only wish I had thought of it first."

Toward the end of December, Rodrigo became a hunter of rats. Thin, with ash-gray shadows around his eyes, he would disappear into the hold like a fox down a hole and not return until he held a rat by the tail.

I went with him once. I crouched beside him, surrounded by darkness, the buzz of flies, the stench and heat so thick I could scarce breathe. We waited for what seemed hours. Then, suddenly, Rodrigo hurled a chunk of iron into the darkness. "Got him!" he shrieked. A moment later, he proudly held the carcass before my eyes. "A pregnant female. Worth even more, for she is extra tender and tasty."

Many of us turned away from the rats, refusing to eat them. We hated them as much as we hated the cockroaches that erupted out of the bilges each night, scurrying over us while we slept.

To begin with, Rodrigo did not make much money, and a rat sold for only a few pennies. But as the food supply dwindled, we became insane, cursing and fighting to be the highest bidder. One rat sold for a golden ducat. At first we skinned them, eating only their soft pink flesh, hating the way they stuck in our throats with nothing but piss to wash them down. Soon we became like savages, eating the rats fur, bones, and all. At the start of his rat trade, Rodrigo would give me a portion of the rat—a leg, the tail—for free. But as the rats became more valuable and our hunger increased until we lived with constant pain, he ceased to give me rats. For many days I despised him.

Then one day Rodrigo disappeared into the hold and did not return.

XVIII

January 9—March 6, 1521

I opened my swollen mouth and hollered into the darkness.

Nothing.

I sucked in clean air, held my breath, and descended into the hold, a lantern in my hand. Rodrigo had been beaten. He lay between casks of cargo, his face a mass of bruises, his eyes swollen shut. Blood seeped from his mouth.

"Rodrigo!" I cried. I set the lantern down and knelt beside him, raising his head into my arms. It no longer mattered that I despised him. He was my best friend.

He opened his mouth, his gums crimson and swollen. "I didn't even see him, Mateo. He came from nowhere."

I heaved him over my shoulder and carried him from the hold. I laid him on his bedding, wiping his bruised eyes with a rag moistened with salt water. Hours later I dreamed of Rodrigo's crazed eyes. I dreamed of the veins in his throat, bulging as he struggled to breathe, of a rat half thrust down his mouth. I dreamed that the tiny feet scrabbled against his chin, the tail whipping his cheeks. Nightmares. Always nightmares.

From that day forward, Rodrigo was out of business. Bigger, stronger men now roamed the hold, slugging senseless anyone who dared to enter.

The supply of biscuit rapidly dwindled. If it could be called biscuit, for it was yellow, filled with rat piss, crumbling into a powder that heaved with worms and weevil. We had not even shark flesh to fill our bellies. Come the New Year, they had ceased to swarm about our ships.

We hated what we saw. We looked at one another and saw only hunger. We were humans turned animals. And we looked away, for each of us knew he gazed at his own reflection. No longer did we lower the sails by night for we were too weak. It mattered not. Day after day the wind did not change and blew steady from our quarter, and though there was nothing but the endless sea, we made good speed.

One day we lay on the deck, mouths slack, watching as Magallanes tossed some charts into the sea. He screamed and tore his clothing. "With the pardon of the mapmakers, the Spice Islands are not to be found at their appointed place!" I blankly realized that his clothes hung upon his starved frame like a tent on a pole. I realized that for many days he had not called for me to sing to him. That for many days I had not set foot in his cabin.

I had forgotten. Hunger had dulled everything.

That evening, I stumbled into the captain-general's cabin. It was moist as a jungle. Enrique lay curled in a corner like a dog asleep, stinking in a puddle of his own filth. The room was a shambles. Maps, charts, books, parchments, writing supplies, and nautical instruments lay scattered between boots and dirtied clothing.

Magallanes lay on his bed, his beard wild and untrimmed, his eyes closed in hollow, sunken sockets. At first I thought he was dead, and it reminded me of something so long ago, of someone I loved. An ache filled my heart.

I began to clean. I propped a sword in a corner and cleared the table. I tossed garbage overboard. I ate the crumbs. I rolled charts and folded clothes that reeked of sweat. Suddenly, I saw a movement out of the corner of my eye. I stopped folding clothes, staring. On the wall hung a mirror. I blinked, confused. From deep within the mirror, a desperate stranger stared back. Distorted. Horrifying. Running his tongue over cracked lips.

God, no.

Slowly, bones creaking, I covered the mirror with a shirt, thankful when the stranger vanished. I wished the dizziness behind my eyes would go away as well. I wished the raspy, persistent voice hammering in my head would shut up and leave me alone.

God has abandoned me, it said again and again. *God has abandoned me. Do you hear, Mateo? God has abandoned me. We are lost. All of us, lost.* And the voice wept.

The food was gone.

We stripped the leather from the yardarms and soaked it in seawater to soften it. This we ate with a gruel made from sawdust.

"This is tasty," said Rodrigo, chewing.

I said nothing, forcing myself to swallow.

"Are you going to draw this in your sketchbook, Mateo? Us sitting and eating leather and sawdust soup?"

"Maybe I will."

"Maybe I will eat your sketchbook."

"Maybe I will stab you with my quill."

"What will we eat next, do you think? How about some rigging? How about some nails?" Rodrigo snorted. "Do you know, Mateo, this would be funny were I not so hungry. I heard of a man who was so hungry he chopped off his legs and ate them. And then his fingers. But once his fingers were gone, he couldn't chop off his arms because he couldn't hold his knife anymore. He did everything in the wrong order, you see, so then he had to gnaw—"

"Stop it, Rodrigo. You solve nothing with such talk."

He stared at me, his eyes crazy again. Did I look the same? My hair stinking and matted, my face whiskered and filthy, my gums swollen, my teeth rotten and loose, flies crawling in and out of every crevice. I turned away.

Rodrigo talked to the back of my head. "Don't you see, Mateo? This is the end. Magallanes has killed us all. Even himself."

I clamped my hands over my ears.

Day after blistering day.

Hell.

We crowded into the shade, panting, groaning with every move. Some men were mere bones, thumping the deck whenever they rolled over, a hollow clacking, sticks upon a drum. Others swelled like pregnant sows, bloated, crying with pain. All of us were surrounded by putrefying stink.

We waited.

To see who would be next.

Swellings covered my body. Colorful swellings—red, blue, yellow, green—each the size of a nut. Sometimes the swellings opened, oozing with juices. Miserable, I begged my mother to pray for me. To take the pain away. Pretending she pressed a damp cloth to my face. . . .

"O my Jesus," I hear her pray, "forgive us our sins, save us from the fires of hell and lead all souls to heaven, especially those who are in most need of Thy mercy." Then her voice softens and tears fill her eyes. "*Ave Maria, gratia plena, Dominus tecum. Benedicta tu in mulieribus, et benedictus fructus ventris tui, Iesus. Sancta Maria, Mater Dei, ora pro nobis peccatoribus, nunc, et in hora mortis nostrae. Amen.*"

Again and again she says this prayer. . . .

I never knew she could speak Latin.

One night someone stumbled against me.

I gasped with pain, opening my eyes. A shape loomed over me in the darkness. It is Death, I thought dully. Death has come to fetch me.

Death grabbed me and yanked me to my feet. My every joint screamed with agony. "I have done it," it breathed. The stench of rottenness wafted over me. "Come, Mateo. Come." It pulled me through the darkness into a cabin. A single lantern burned upon a table next to a map and an astrolabe made of brass.

"I have done it," it said again. It pointed to the map. "There is an island out there. I saw it. It is big, and there is food and water." Death looked at me then. Crazed. Shrunken.

Magallanes . . .

"An island?" My voice like sand, dry, grainy. I approached the map slowly. It was drawn on creamy paper, crinkled with use. Rivers of blue snaked through the land. Letters of gilded gold. Names of cities.

Seville. Málaga.

It was a map of Spain.

He pointed to Castile. "We will arrive tomorrow," he was saying, his voice high-pitched and feverish. "You must tell the crew. Tell them we've arrived and to prepare." He knelt and raised his face toward the ceiling. "O God Almighty, You have answered the prayers of the weak. O Father, Thou art merciful!"

I crawled back to my sleeping place.

That night I dreamed of an island. Lush, brimming with food and water.

In the morning, my dream came true.

We stood at the bulwarks, crowded together. We leaned on one another, panting, staring. None of us said anything. From behind me came the sound of a sword sliding into its scabbard. Then Magallanes ordered the sheets let fly and the anchor dropped. I heard the shuffle of bare feet. The creak of rigging. The whip of sails loosened. Still, most of us stood and stared.

"We are saved," whispered Rodrigo.

"Aye," I answered.

Thatched huts dotted the beach—an island village. A sea of canoes headed toward us. The natives paddled hard, their muscles shining and straining. They pulled alongside, seeming unafraid. Still we stared.

"Perhaps they have food," said Rodrigo, spitting a tooth from his mouth even as he spoke.

The native men swarmed aboard. They were tall, well built, handsome, with stone knives and bone-tipped spears and shields tufted with human hair. With cries of astonishment, they fell upon our metalworks, our buckets, and our weapons.

We stood and stared.

One savage lifted a hatchet and sniffed its iron head. He scratched and tapped it with his finger, then licked it. He grunted and stuffed it under his arm to grab another. They filled their arms with stools, clothing, knives.

"Do you have any food?" a shipmate asked, his voice breaking.

The natives ignored him. A kettle. A hammer. A pike.

"Please!" Magallanes held out his arms in an effort to stop them. His arms were bone thin, browned by the sun. "We come in peace. We have brought many items for trade, but you must put down those things you have taken. We need them, and they do not belong to you."

The natives smiled and nodded, their teeth stained black and red.

A native approached me. His gaze traveled from my head to my toes. Then, before I could stop him, he snatched my rosary from my hand, smiling his black-and-red smile. I opened my mouth to scream "Give that back!" but all that came from my mouth was a gasp and a croak. I fell to my knees, weakened, my heart hammering.

"Marines, gird yourselves in armor!" I heard Magallanes say. "Espinosa, clear the decks of natives and retrieve all they have stolen."

It was a shipwide effort to dress the marines in armor. Each marine was too weak to do it himself. The natives watched, talking excitedly. One stepped forward and tapped on Espinosa's armor as if he were knocking upon a door.

Dressed in their shining armor, looking once again like soldiers of Spain, proud and unconquerable, the marines began to take back the items from the natives—a hatchet, a harquebus—while the natives blinked in surprise, their hands now empty. Then, suddenly, the natives turned fierce and shoved the marines away. One marine lost his balance and collapsed. His helmet clattered to the deck. And while I watched, stupefied, two natives kicked him senseless.

The captain-general's hand sliced through the air as a signal.

Espinosa fired his crossbow and struck an island chief in the shoulder. The natives gasped. The chief dropped his stolen belongings in surprise and stared at the protruding arrow. He withdrew it from his shoulder in utter amazement while Espinosa fired another cross-bolt into his chest. Blood spewed out of the native's mouth and he crumpled slowly to the deck.

Now the air thickened with screams and cross-bolts. The deck grew sticky with blood. The natives leaped aboard their canoes, but not before we had slain six of them.

"They have stolen our skiff!" cried Magallanes. "Fire a broadside into their village!"

Cannon boomed and huts disintegrated in a spray of leaves, sticks, and grass. Forty armed marines piled into the longboat and went ashore. They destroyed canoes and scoured the deserted village for food.

"We shall soon eat," I whispered to Rodrigo as we peered over the gunwale.

"Aye. I would destroy a thousand villages just to eat again."

It seemed forever before the marines returned with fresh water, chickens, pigs, fruit such as none I'd seen before, rice, yams, and, of course, the skiff. The pigs still squealed as I spitted them and thrust them over the fires, my mouth watering, my hands shaking.

Such an orgy of feasting! Pork falling from the bone. Roasted yams. The tender breasts of chickens. Fruit bursting with juices. Fresh, sweet-smelling water. We ate and ate and drank and drank. For the first time in weeks, I heard laughter and conversation. Grease smeared my fingers and chin. My gums stung from the fruits. I lost a tooth in a yam. One of my sores burst open, dribbling with pus.

It was the happiest day of my life.

We sailed from island to island like hungry bees.

Water here. Food there.

Graves dotted the beaches as men still died of plague, food or not. For myself, I grew strong. Rodrigo, too. We clasped each other's hands, laughing. The worst was behind us.

One day as we made our way through a string of islands, I swabbed the floor as the captain-general studied his charts, as he grunted now and then, his breath whistling through his nostrils. He had grown stronger, too. His frame had filled out, and he no longer had that shrunken, starved look. He hurriedly dipped his quill into the ink pot and then wrote, paused, and wrote, the quill flying across the paper like a summer storm.

I approached the table slowly, wondering. "Do you know where we are?"

"Not now, Mateo."

"Are we almost there? At the Spice Islands, I mean?"

"Mateo, please. I have much on my mind."

I chewed my fingernail, bursting with questions. "Do you think we'll return home to Spain? Someday, I mean?"

He did not answer me. Instead he scooped up his charts and

left the cabin so abruptly the flame sputtered in the lantern and went out.

It was then I noticed the shadows move. Enrique.

For the entire voyage, I had heard Enrique speak but a few words and only to Magallanes. Now for the first time, he spoke to me, his voice high and girl-like. "The gods have chosen him."

"Excuse me?"

"My master. He is a great man. To sail away in one direction and arrive home from another. Such a thing has never been done before."

I blinked. "How do you know this? Did he say we had traveled around the world?"

Enrique's eyes glinted. "Because I can understand the language of the islands. I am home."

For a moment I did not understand. Then I remembered something Rodrigo had told me. Many years ago Enrique had been captured as a slave by Magallanes during a campaign in the Far East. "You mean, we are in the Far East? That means the Spice Islands are . . ." My voice trailed away when I realized the shadows were empty. I was alone.

I finished swabbing the floor.

It was true what Enrique said. Soon everyone on the ship knew it—that we had arrived in the Far East by sailing west. Magallanes had achieved the impossible! Excitement gripped us like a fever. Soon, we knew, we would arrive at the Spice Islands. Gold, jewels, spices, pearls. Then it would be home for Spain, our ships staggering under the weight of our wealth, the glory of our fame.

"God has indeed blessed this man with greatness," some whispered, speaking of Magallanes.

"Aye," whispered others. "Cartagena could never have done such a thing."

Even Rodrigo did not have a ready retort, knowing, for once, that what everyone said was true. Our captain-general was a great man.

Island after island, the fleet now well fed and provisioned, Magallanes made peace with the natives, using Enrique as the interpreter. Magallanes brought chiefs aboard and presented them with fine gifts: Turkish robes and Spanish hats, mirrors and knives. His face flushed with pride, he showed them how the sails were raised and lowered. He spread out his charts and compasses, explaining how we had sailed across one ocean, found a strait through a continent, and then crossed another great ocean to these islands.

Then, always, without warning, the cannon roared, belching flame, throwing the chiefs to the ground. Magallanes raised them, saying we mean no harm. But we all knew. Even the chiefs knew. It was a show of force. We wanted our power understood by all. We stood watching, our arms crossed, knowing none could defeat us. Not with their puny sticks and stones. Not while Magallanes was our captain-general.

The natives were then treated to a mock battle, staged between a fully armored Espinosa and three men armed only with swords and daggers. Espinosa had no trouble fighting them off. We enjoyed watching the chiefs' eyes widen with fear.

"We have two hundred such armed men on each of our ships," Magallanes always boasted, his voice ringing with triumph. "One armed Spaniard would be worth one hundred of your fighting men. There is no one in the world who can defeat us!"

At night I slept soundly. I am Mateo Macías, a Spaniard, a conqueror. There are none who can defeat us.

XX

March 30–April 26, 1521

Late one night, after an exhausting day of chiefs and treaties, the captain-general requested to see my drawings. I hurried to his cabin, anxious to please him.

His brows drawn together, he studied my sketchbook. There were drawings of the strait, the seabirds, sharks, men dying of plague, island chiefs. There was a drawing of Magallanes himself. In the sketch, he sat in a chair, brooding, his face troubled and distracted. "I look like this?" he asked.

"Aye. Sometimes."

There was another drawing of him. Bone-thin. Starving. I saw him scowl as he studied this drawing. For a long time I heard nothing but his breathing. In. Out. He traced the edges of the figure, as if by doing so he could feel its flesh, as if he were remembering what it was like to be this hungry person. Finally he asked, "Have you heard of Job?"

Without waiting for my reply, he went on, "Job was a goodly man who honored God. He had everything one could wish for in this world, and each day he worshiped God in thankfulness. God blessed him with great wealth, and Job had many sons and daughters. One day God decided to test Job. He afflicted Job with much suffering."

I had, in fact, heard this story many times from my mother. "God took Job's family from him and destroyed Job's wealth. And then He gave Job a terrible disease, like the plague."

Magallanes nodded. "Job suffered terribly, as we have suffered. Of course, Job was angry at God for his afflictions, believing he was a righteous man and that righteous men should not suffer. But in that thought alone, Job sinned, believing himself wiser than the Almighty. Once he realized this, Job repented."

"He passed the test." I wondered why the captain-general was telling me this story.

"Aye, he passed the test. As I shall pass mine."

"Sir?"

Magallanes did not answer. Instead he brushed his beard, seemingly lost in thought. I wondered if I should leave, if I should speak.

Then he stood, my drawing clutched in his hand. He strode to the covered mirror and pulled off the shirt. The shirt fell to the floor, exposing the mirror for the first time in weeks. A film of green slime covered the surface. He swiped his hand across the glass and as he did so, I glimpsed his reflection in the cloudy green smear. His breath upon the glass. And in the depths of his brown eyes, I saw something I'd never seen before. A fire. Burning.

He stared at himself. "The scales have fallen from my eyes," he murmured, sighing. "My heart is full." He pressed his palm against the mirrored surface as my drawing floated to his feet, forgotten.

161

" 'For I know that my Redeemer lives and that at the last He will stand upon the earth; and after my skin has been thus destroyed, then in my flesh I shall see God.' "

Warmth crept into my face and I shifted my feet. When he said no more, I gathered my drawings and left.

We were a happy crew, on our way to gold and riches.

We had been told by local chieftains that Humabon, the chief of Cebu, was the chief of all chiefs. While Magallanes wanted a treaty with this man—peace and lands in the name of Spain—the crew wanted riches. There were gold nuggets the size of hens' eggs to be found in Cebu, we'd been told, even the size of ostrichs' eggs, maybe.

"Soon, Mateo," said Rodrigo, "our sea chests will overflow with gold. They will be so heavy we will have to use an elephant to carry them."

"You have seen an elephant?"

"No, but I hear they are taller than a building and can carry gold easily."

"Ah," I sighed, trying to imagine such a creature.

On the sixth day of April, we approached the island of Cebu. Fishing villages dotted the shores. Their houses were constructed of boards and logs, elevated off the ground with pilings. Hogs, chickens, and goats rooted for food and slept under the shade of the huts. Out of doorways tumbled scores of natives, pointing at our ships. Boys and men jumped into outrigger canoes and followed us. The canoe sails were of different colors, and by nightfall, a rainbow of a thousand colors sailed in our wake.

On the morning of April 7, 1521, one year after the execution of Quesada, we hove to in the bay of the bustling port city of Cebu. The squadron's gunners fired a salute.

"See how they run and hide?" Rodrigo pointed. "Nothing can match the power and might of Spaniards."

A delegation representing Humabon came aboard the flagship to begin negotiations for a treaty of peace between the Spaniards and the island of Cebu.

Again a staged combat was performed.

Afterward, Magallanes reassured them. "You have nothing to fear from the Spanish power, for our weapons are soft to our friends and rough to our enemies; and as a cloth wipes away the sweat from a man, so our weapons destroy the enemies of our faith."

Then before us all, the captain-general dropped to his knees and prayed. When he finished, he held out his hands to the natives and urged them to accept the Christian faith. "My fleet padre can baptize you this day."

The natives were silent and I saw they did not know what to do. Perhaps they did not yet understand baptism, though the captain-general had explained it again and again.

Confronted with their silence, Magallanes continued, "I beg of you, do not become Christians only because I tell you or because you fear the power of the Spaniards. Become Christians because you know in your hearts this is the right thing to do. I plead with each of you to consider this deeply, to search your souls. And to those that choose this day to become a Christian, I will give a full suit of Spanish armor."

The delegation conferred before the prince spoke. "We accept your treaty of peace and give you our assurances that Rajah

163

Humabon will be delighted as well. We desire to become Christians and each of us wishes to be baptized today."

Magallanes embraced each of them. "By my faith in God, by my loyalty to the king, and by the crusader's habit I wear, I swear perpetual peace will exist between the kings of Spain and the kings of Cebu."

Over the next two weeks, Rajah Humabon and all his household, his wives and his children, were baptized. In a colorful ceremony in the town's square, eight hundred native people knelt before the cross, repented of their sins, and turned their lives to God.

Then, in a token of friendship, Magallanes offered his men, his ships, and all his weapons if Humabon had any enemies that refused to recognize his rule. Humabon, a short fat brown man—covered with tattoos and naked except for a breechcloth—said there were several nearby chiefs who refused to submit to his authority. Immediately Magallanes ordered messengers dispatched. "Tell them if they refuse to recognize Humabon's authority, they and all their villages will suffer death and we shall seize their property."

Soon after, a flood of dignitaries from surrounding islands arrived with their households, each desiring to be baptized. They had heard of the god of the Spaniards. They brought tribute, knelt, and pledged their loyalty to Spain while holy water rained upon their heads. In all, more than two thousand people converted to Christianity.

During this time, we rented a trading post from Rajah Humabon and stocked it with goods. The natives brought their silk, their precious stones, goats, chickens, pigs, sugarcane, ginger, and pearls to trade for copper bracelets, bells, quicksilver, mirrors, fishhooks, combs, metal basins, bolts of cotton fabric, velvet, satin, and fine lace.

But it was not chickens we wanted, it was gold. And it was not fine lace they wanted, but iron and bronze. A firm price was established. For ten weights of gold, each valued at a ducat and a half, the islanders received fourteen pounds of iron. So successful was this trade that Magallanes forbade us to trade for gold, lest the ships be stripped of iron in our craze for wealth.

At first I obeyed the captain-general's orders, scowling as Rodrigo traded a handful of nails for a nugget of gold. Rodrigo saw me watching and spat. "You are a fool, Mateo. The captain-general is made blind by his desire to baptize all the natives and sees nothing else." He spat again. "I tell you, if he continues in his zeal, we shall none of us see the Spice Islands. It is what everyone is saying. So I shall make my riches now, for it may be my only chance. You would be wise to do the same, Mateo. Put your foolish honesty aside. It will serve only to make you a poor man."

The next day, alone in the captain-general's cabin, before I could stop myself, I took an astrolabe—a beautiful brass one with intricate designs—and shoved it down my shirt. I hid it in my sea chest, intending to trade it on the morrow, shame burning my chest like fire. It is only one astrolabe, I told myself. The captain-general has many. Besides, I cannot die poor.

That evening, to my dismay, Magallanes called for me to sing to him. I attacked my guitar and sang boisterously, hoping in my loudness I could drown the sounds of shame. He watched me, silently, lifting his eyebrow as if wondering who this wild boy was who sat before me.

Relief washed through me when he waved his hand to dismiss me. But before I could hurry away, he stood and tilted his face upward, his arms outstretched like an angel's. " 'If you return to the Almighty,' " he whispered, " 'you will be restored . . . if you treat gold like dust and gold of Ophir like the stones of the torrent-bed, and if the Almighty is your gold and your precious silver, then you will delight yourself in the Almighty, and lift up your face to God.' "

Then he looked at me. In that moment, horrified, I knew he knew.

That night, I dreamed of fire and hell and of my mother's voice saying over and over, *Thou shalt not steal. Thou shalt not steal.*

The next day I returned the astrolabe to where I had found it.

"It was foolish to return it," said Rodrigo later, shaking his head as we sat together under the shade of a palm tree. "He has many others—you said so yourself. You could have sold it for ten nuggets of gold. Twenty, maybe. I guess you cannot help being foolish. It is in your nature, just as it is in mine to die a rich man."

"Shut up, Rodrigo," I said, glad I had returned it. "I would rather die a poor man than a thief. Besides, it will not matter that I am poor. I will live with you in your castle. We are brothers, are we not? Is that not what brothers do?"

Rodrigo studied me a moment. Then, to my surprise, he drew his dagger. "Brothers? You think we are brothers?" And while my mouth dropped with shock, Rodrigo drew his knife across the flesh of his forearm. Instantly blood welled and trickled down his arm. "Go ahead," he said. "You're next. We shall become brothers in blood. We shall prove our loyalty to each other."

I hesitated only a moment with my own dagger before I cut

deep, trying not to wince with the sudden, sharp pain. Smearing our hands with blood, we clasped each other's hands in a firm grip.

"Blood brothers forever," Rodrigo whispered.

"Blood brothers forever," I echoed.

Nothing would separate us, we vowed. Nothing but death itself.

One day I spied Espinosa praying. I paused and peered through the crack of his cabin door, astonished to see him kneeling on the floor with his hands clasped. I had never seen Espinosa pray before.

"Come in," he said without opening his eyes.

Embarrassed to have been caught spying, I entered the cabin, the floorboards creaking beneath my feet, closing the door behind me. The cabin was not nearly so luxurious or large as the captain-general's, but it was tidy. Spartan. I sat upon his bunk, my face hot.

He opened his eyes and looked at me. Suddenly he seemed exhausted. The knowledge surprised me, for I had thought of Espinosa as the strongest among the strong, tireless. "I am not a praying man," he said simply.

I said nothing, waiting.

"I thought getting on my knees would be enough. It is not. I am bereft of words. Besides, God does not speak to men such as me."

"Why not?"

Espinosa said nothing for a while, his eyes the color of cool waters. "Does He speak to you, Mateo?"

I searched for an answer. "Sometimes I think I hear Him. In the wind, maybe. In the stars at night. I don't know."

The master-at-arms looked away and sighed. "I fear we are in trouble, Mateo."

"What do you mean?"

"Today Magallanes discovered some of the natives offering sacrifices before their idols. When he confronted them, they told him that the brother of the prince was sick and they were sacrificing for his recovery."

"Was he angry?"

"More saddened than angry. He told them that it was because of their unbelief that the man was ill. That if they would only believe in Jesus Christ, the man would be made well. To prove his point, he said that if the man was not made whole that very hour, they could strike the captain-general's head from his body."

I gasped. "And?"

"Upon reaching the sick man's house, Magallanes ordered him to rise and talk, and the man did so. He was healed. The island rejoices, but I cannot." He shook his head, the strain evident upon his face. "Ever since we arrived at Cebu and began baptizing natives—hundreds of them, then thousands—a terrible feeling has settled upon me, as if this is somehow wrong. As if—as if—" Espinosa struggled for words. "I don't know, Mateo. But for the first time in my life, I am afraid."

Again I said nothing, my heart suddenly hammering.

"Pray with me, Mateo. Kneel beside me and find the words that elude me. Pray with me."

So I prayed with Espinosa. But instead of peace, a terrible uneasiness grew within me, wormlike and crawling. As I prayed, thunder rumbled in the distance. And when I uttered "Amen," it began to rain.

For days this uneasiness did not leave me. Instead it grew stronger, clutching my heart with the same icy hand that clutched Espinosa's.

I watched and listened as Magallanes went ashore each day to extol the doctrines of Christianity. He spoke of the Trinity, the Immaculate Conception, Adam and Eve, and honoring one's father and mother. The padre baptized so many people that, come nightfall each day, he lacked strength to raise his arms in blessing. And with each baptism, my unease mounted. As if the stage were set. The actors poised to begin. I knew not what to make of my feelings, whether they be imagination or warning, and so, unsure, I did nothing. Said nothing.

Then, one evening, the curtains opened and the play began.

A nearby chieftain refused to pay tribute to Rajah Humabon. With a wave of his hand, Magallanes dispatched Espinosa and his marines, who burned the chieftain's village and returned to the flagship with livestock and plunder. Magallanes sent messengers once again. "Tell all the chiefs who refuse baptism and who refuse to recognize Humabon's authority that the same arm that struck this village will strike them also."

One of the messengers returned. Even before he spoke, I knew what he would say. "My captain-general, the chieftain of the island of Mactan has this message for you. He refuses to be baptized into the religion of strangers. He refuses to pay tribute to Humabon, a man he despises. He says that if the Spaniards come to burn his village, he will be waiting for them."

Enraged, Magallanes stormed the deck. All night I listened to his uneven steps, unable to sleep, imagining that strange glare in his eyes that I had seen of late. My skin turned icy and my insides crawled. When the next day he called the crew together, I stood before him with my shipmates, the planks of the deck hot beneath my feet.

The final act.

"The wrath of God is terrible and His divine purpose among these islanders will not be thwarted!" He spat his words and his eyes gleamed and he was frightful to behold. "Tomorrow, prepare to invade Mactan! We will force the ruler to his knees. And on his knees he will taste Spanish steel!"

XXI
April 27, 1521

Midnight.

A stark slice of moon.

Stars white as salt.

The soft slap of water.

My hands, sweaty already, pulled against the oars.

From the shore of Cebu, a bird cawed, its cry shattering the stillness. Dogs began to bark.

"It is an evil omen," Enrique whispered, his dark face hidden in the night.

We pulled away from the island of Cebu and started across the narrow channel separating Cebu from Mactan. The barking of the dogs followed us, seemingly forever, barking, barking, until finally, after perhaps an hour, there was silence. Naught but the slap of oars.

Twenty of us bunched together in one of three longboats. At our feet lay pikes, harquebuses, crossbows, and swords. For myself, when it was not my turn to row, I clutched my crossbow and fingered the edge of my sword. A knotted fear writhed within my bowels. Would I live to see the morrow? Or would the screaming, painted face of a savage be the last I would see? I prayed to the Virgin for courage.

Through the darkness the island of Mactan loomed like a predator hidden in the brush. Rocks jutted like fangs through the waters and we hove to, not daring to row any closer. It would be three hours until daylight. A quick conference was held among the captains of the three longboats and Humabon, who commanded one thousand warriors in thirty large canoes.

It was decided. We would wait until dawn. The shore was too treacherous to navigate under cover of darkness.

I shivered. While we waited, a light mist descended. Coldness seeped into me, slithering beneath my armor like a serpent. Mosquitoes plagued me, biting my face, my neck, my hands, and I swatted them constantly.

I looked to the prow of the longboat where the captain-general sat. Oblivious to the insects, he stared unmoving and unblinking at the dark mass of land.

When Magallanes had announced his intention to attack Mactan, there had been immediate and loud opposition. The other two captains, Serrano and a young man with a jagged scar across his nose, had pleaded with the captain-general to reconsider. "Our mission is not to meddle in the local affairs of natives," cried Serrano, his older, softened features suddenly turning hard. "We are not missionaries. We are not settlers of new colonies. We have been commissioned by the king to seek the Spice Islands and to bring home spices."

The younger captain agreed and called the mission foolhardy. "Remember the fate of the explorer devoured by cannibals! You should not leave your ships for such an unimportant venture. The loss of our commander would devastate our voyage. I beg you to reconsider!"

"Silence! I will hear no opposition! I refuse to listen while you sow seeds of fear and cowardice! Did God lead us so far only to desert us now? Are we to quail when faced with battle? Did Moses submit to Pharaoh? Did David quake before the Philistines? With God on our side, we cannot fail!"

"I refuse to be party to such a venture!" cried Serrano.

"I also refuse," said the scar-nosed captain, "and I urge you most vehemently to forsake this madness."

Magallanes's face twisted with fury. "Madness? You dare to call God's holy work madness? Upon my honor and with God's holy sword, I tell you that were I to have a handful of untried men, boys even, I could defeat one hundred times their number."

"You would be annihilated," said Serrano. He sounded tired, beaten.

"It is impossible for an army of God to be annihilated!" Magallanes roared, his eyes aflame, and in that moment I was terrified of him. "And to prove it, I shall have no man by my side who does not volunteer, who does not willingly side with me, knowing that I do the work of God Almighty."

"That is insane!" cried the younger captain.

"None!" Magallanes bellowed. "Even Espinosa and his marines will remain behind! I will prove to you that even with an army of untried men, we shall show these natives the power of our might. With a few we shall conquer many, and when we are victorious, none shall dare oppose Humabon. These islands shall belong to Spain. There shall be none mightier than the king!"

Espinosa pushed his way forward through the crew. "Captain-General, please, you must listen. I cannot allow you to follow such madness. I will lead the battle. You must stay with—"

"Do not speak to me of madness! We cannot fail! Do you understand me? Failure is impossible when we are led by God's holy light and the presence of the Divine Virgin! With my cross and my sword I shall prevail!"

When Humabon heard of the impending attack on Mactan, he also begged Magallanes to reconsider. And when Magallanes again refused, Humabon said, "Let me attack Mactan first with a thousand of my best warriors. We know their defenses. We know the look and feel of the island in the darkness. When we signal, then you come with your armed men. They will be fresh and ready to fight. In this way we will defeat Mactan."

Magallanes had bowed before Humabon. "My honored friend, you may bring your thousand warriors, but I forbid them to leave their canoes. You must keep out of battle. And from the comfort of your canoes, Rajah Humabon, you and your warriors will see how Spaniards fight. You will see how our enemies scatter before us like chaff in the wind."

A fighting force of sixty volunteers was assembled. Barbers, cabin boys, seamen, dignitaries. Men who had never before fired a crossbow or a harquebus. Men who had never before held a sword while it pierced the body of another.

As I had hurried across the waist deck to fetch a suit of armor from Espinosa, I saw Rodrigo. He stood bare-chested, his feet wide apart, swinging a broadsword from side to side, grunting with the effort. The air whistled as the blade sliced up and down.

"Then you are going, too?" I had asked, surprised.

"Yes, I am going."

"But why?"

Rodrigo ignored me, saying nothing, still swinging the sword. Finally he stopped, glistening with sweat. His chest heaved. He looked at me then, as serious as I had ever seen him. "Because the captain-general has gone mad."

I said nothing.

"Because, mad or not, he has led us this far, and if I let him go into battle without my sword to protect him, then I am not a man. A man of honor, anyway."

I blinked, stunned.

He peered down the length of his sword, as if to check its straightness. He ran a finger along its edge. "Besides," he continued, his mouth curving into a half grin, "I can't let you have all the adventure, can I?"

A lump grew in my throat as we clasped hands.

"I'll watch your back, brother," he said.

"Aye, and I yours."

Later Espinosa helped me into my armor. His face looked harsh in the lantern light, and when he spoke, his voice broke, as if already grieved. "Stay by the captain-general's side, Mateo. Protect him at all costs. Put all doubts aside. This is battle and you are a warrior. Do not hesitate to kill. Remember, Mateo. You are a warrior."

You are a warrior . . . you are a warrior . . .

Red-orange streaks of light.

The stink of fear.

The creak of the boat.

The clank of steel.

Rodrigo across from me. Knuckles bone white against the hilt of his sword. Forehead beaded with perspiration.

With a wave of his hand, Magallanes said, "Take the longboats in as far as you can."

The longboats moved—silent, gliding birds—into a small bay, leaving the canoes of Humabon and his thousand warriors behind. Forbidden by Magallanes to enter into combat, they would observe the battle from a distance. In the shelter of the bay a village slept, unaware.

Still far from shore, the longboats' passage blocked by a coral reef, Magallanes ordered us to drop anchor. "The tide is too low. From here we walk. Remove your leg armor."

After doing his bidding, I dropped into the sea. Water lapped around my thighs, cool at first, quickly turning warm. Rodrigo handed me my weapons and then lowered himself into the water.

In the pale light of dawn, forty-eight men followed Magallanes. The gunners stayed in the longboats to provide covering fire from the swivel guns. None of us spoke, but we all knew that once we reached but halfway to shore, we would be out of range of the swivel guns. I wondered why we had not waited for high tide.

It took us an eternity to wade to shore in the dim morning light. My legs grew heavy. I stumbled over coral, sharp as daggers, hidden beneath the shallows. Under my armor, moisture drenched my clothing, whether from sweat or from the splashing of water I knew not. My breath came in gasps and the thud of my heart sounded in my ears.

We reached shore silently, without opposition. Magallanes waited until all forty-eight men stood on the beach.

Then he ordered the village burned.

A seaman lit a torch and set the first hut ablaze. It caught quickly and the flames snapped and black smoke roiled as the seaman ran to the next hut. And the next. Soon, twenty huts burned like giant torches and still we saw no natives. The village was deserted.

As the seaman thrust his torch into yet another hut, a black object hurtled toward him. I stared while he staggered back and fell, an arrow protruding from his throat.

Immediately the woods to either side of us erupted with natives. They poured toward us like flame, their mouths open, screaming, terrifying. All became bedlam. Chaos. The whine of arrows. The crack of armor. The snap of crossbows. Screams of dying men. Stones falling like rain. The deafening roar in my ears. The smell of blood, sharp, sickening. My own fear. Knotted. Writhing in my bowels.

O Mother Mary! God in Heaven!

There were hundreds of them. Thousands.

"Retreat! Retreat!" cried Magallanes. He began to back away from the village toward the beach. He slashed at the natives with giant swings of his sword. Along with Rodrigo, Enrique, and several others, I flanked his side. Loaded my crossbow. Fired. Again. Again.

We reached the water. I ran out of crossbow bolts and tossed away the crossbow, pulling my sword from its sheath. I held it in front of me with both hands. *Protect him at all costs. You are a warrior.*

I glanced behind us, toward the waiting longboats, and what I saw caused my heart to freeze with horror. The rest of our men, twenty, thirty of them, had fled in panic. Already they were halfway to the longboats. "Cowards!" I screamed to their backs. "Cowards!"

By now the natives knew which one was our leader. They hurled their spears at Magallanes, and when the weapons glanced off his armor, they picked up their spears and hurled them again.

Back we stumbled into the water. Warmth lapped around my knees.

They knocked off the captain-general's helmet. I fetched it from the water and thrust it back on his head. My arms wearied. My muscles screamed. Still I raised my sword and slashed.

You are a warrior.

Out of the corner of my eye, I saw a flash. Heard a strangled cry. Then Rodrigo went down. A spear through his throat. I screamed, dropped my sword, and fell by his side. "Rodrigo!" I raised his head from the water. "He's drowning! He's drowning!" A wisp of blood spilled from around the spear.

"He is dead! Leave him! Re—" The voice of Magallanes cut off as an arrow pierced his thigh. He cursed with pain. "Mateo!" he gasped. "Retreat! I order you!"

I cried with anguish and laid Rodrigo back into the water. As I fished for my sword, a blow hit me on the back of my head, knocking my helmet away. Another blow, and the waters beneath me swirled in a haze of blue.

Someone grabbed me from behind and pulled me to my feet. Into my hands someone thrust a sword. Again I swung. Again. And with each swing I screamed like a man gone mad.

A man fighting in front of Magallanes twirled around suddenly, and a strange light entered his eyes. With a creak of armor, he crumpled to the waters and sank beneath them.

Magallanes bellowed like a bull and his sword flashed and the head of the native who had slain this man splattered into two pieces. Magallanes charged through the natives, away from the longboats, screaming for us to retreat.

Protect him at all costs!

I lurched toward him, but I was too late.

A flash of light.

A spear.

It flew through the air and struck the captain-general in the face. At the same time a native slashed Magallanes's leg with a knife and he fell into the water. "Retreat!" was the last word we heard him cry.

I screamed.

Someone grabbed my arm. "Mateo! Hurry, or we will all be slain!"

As I followed, stumbling over coral, lurching toward the longboats, I glanced over my shoulder. A swarm of natives surrounded our captain-general, savagely thrusting their spears into his throat, his legs, his arms. Again a wail of anguish burst from my throat.

Magallanes was dead.

I lay in a stupor.

I lay like a rat on my sleeping mat, breathing the foulness of below deck. My head ached fiercely. Dull throbs, together with sharp, stabbing pain, pierced my skull. The back of my neck burned and swelled from where a poisoned arrow had grazed it.

I did not care.

I tossed upon my mat, listening to the moans of other injured men, realizing that some of the moans came from me, from deep inside. I could not get the image of a young man from my mind.

The hurtling speed of the spear. His strangled, cut-off cry. His face as I raised it from the water. And when I finally fell into a feverish, shivering sleep, still the image was there. The young man's eyes filled with blood. In my dream his lips moved and he begged me to remove the spear. "Please, Mateo, please." I tried to pull the spear from his throat. I pulled and pulled but my arms were too weak. The tide too strong. The water too deep. I could do nothing but let him go and watch him sink beneath the waves, his lips still moving, shedding tears of blood.

I awoke, trembling, crying, chilled with fever. And when I finally pushed the image of the young man from me, another took its place.

A man like my father. Dark, short, limping. A man I loved. He, too, lay injured in the water. He turned toward me, his brooding eyes so sad, so filled with pain, with defeat. He held out his hand and called to me to save him. But when I tried to go to him, someone held me back and I could not move. Then he was surrounded. They beat him and stabbed him. He flailed weakly and then lay still. And the stain in the water blossomed like a crimson flower.

I gasped, awakening.

An injured man beside me groaned. He, too, suffered from the bite of a poisoned arrow, his face so swollen he could not open his eyes. He could scarce open his mouth to talk. "They have taken our light," he cried. Tears dropped from the slits of his eyes to the sleeping mat. "They have taken our comfort, our true guide. Alas, without him we are lost."

Another man lay across from me, his back to the hull. A pain slashed through my skull, sharp and jarring, and I knew his name: Enrique, the slave of Magallanes. He, too, lay wounded, yet he never seemed to sleep. Always, always he stared straight ahead, dry-eyed, at nothing. Perhaps, like me, he suffered from a poison in the heart.

I don't know how long I had lain there—one day, two days, three—when a man with a jagged scar across his nose came to see Enrique. He stood over him with a lantern and we blinked like moles.

He prodded Enrique's ribs with a booted foot. "Get up."

Enrique did nothing, stared at nothing.

"Get up. The fleet is preparing to sail. We need you to negotiate with Humabon for some native pilots to lead us to the Spice Islands."

When Enrique again did nothing, the man cursed and said, "I am captain of the flagship. I am the one who gives the orders now, and you'd do best to follow them."

Enrique said, "I am injured."

"You are not so injured you cannot walk and talk."

Enrique focused on the man who towered above him. "I am no longer a slave. My master wrote in his will that upon his death I was to be freed. As a free man, I choose to stay here and recover from my injury. It is a right afforded any sailor."

The captain cursed. He reached down and savagely grabbed Enrique's neck with one hand. "You think you are a free man?" he snarled. "Think again. I promise upon my soul that when we return to Spain, you will remain a slave to the widow of Magallanes! Not one day will pass in your life in which you can call yourself a free man! Now get out of your filthy bed and obey me or I shall have you flogged before the entire crew!"

A silence hung between them, reeking of hatred. Then, like a ghost rising from its grave, Enrique pushed the captain aside and got to his feet. He swayed slightly. "You will be sorry for this," he hissed before he climbed the companion ladder and left.

The captain stared after him. Then, as if realizing for the first time that we watched him, he smiled and shrugged at us. "One must be firm with slaves, lest they become useless with their whining," he said with a wink.

The next morning, I staggered out on deck, blinking and squinting, unaware until that moment that my cheeks were slick

182

with tears. I wiped my face on my sleeve. Unable to stop myself, I glanced to see if Magallanes paced the quarterdeck, if perhaps Rodrigo stoked the fire in the sandbox, waiting to tell me a great joke. But they were nowhere . . . nowhere. My heart pressed flat, drained.

My captain . . .

My blood brother . . .

Dead . . .

The man with the swollen face stood by the rail. Today I could see his eyes through puffy slits and followed his gaze to where he looked. Several boats, filled with about thirty of our men, had left the ships and now landed at the docks of Cebu.

"Where are they going?" I asked, my voice cracked and hoarse.

"They have been invited ashore for a feast. Rajah Humabon has promised a gift of jewels."

"Jewels?"

"Aye. They were earlier promised to Magallanes. Rubies, diamonds, pearls, gold nuggets even."

Before, such mention of jewels would have made me giddy with wanting. Now, jewels seemed a tarnished possession. I would give all the jewels in the world if it would bring Rodrigo and Magallanes back.

I watched as a delegation from Humabon greeted our crew. Then Serrano, Espinosa, the scar-nosed captain, the padre, and other high-ranking officers disappeared into the city.

The man with the swollen face spoke, "It is said Rajah Humabon cried like a baby when he witnessed Magallanes's death."

My vision clouded and I said nothing, remembering.

"He sat in his canoe with his thousand warriors surrounding him and wept until his tears were gone. He must have loved the captain-general deeply, as did I. It is said he begged the ruler of Mactan to release the body of Magallanes, but the ruler refused, saying he would not give up the body of such a man for anything and that he would display it as a memorial to his triumph."

Smoke from the fires of the great banquet hovered over Cebu. Fishermen, normally gone in their canoes this time of morning, sat motionless on the beach, silent, as if waiting for something. Occasionally one of them glanced at us, gazing at everything from our hull to the pennants hanging lifeless on the halyards high above.

It was then I realized the native children were gone. Normally, they swarmed the shores. Brown-skinned girls and boys surrounded any sailor who stepped ashore, holding out their hands for trinkets. But not today. Today the beaches were silent. A city in mourning.

Suddenly, there appeared on the beach two figures I recognized: Espinosa and a man named Carvalho, the pilot of the *Concepción*. They ran across the beach, climbed into separate skiffs, and began to row—Carvalho to the *Victoria* and Espinosa to the *Trinidad*. When Espinosa climbed aboard, I asked him what was the matter. Why had he returned from the banquet so soon?

"There is something wrong on the island today. Carvalho felt it, too. We've returned for our weapons. We think it might be—"

A sudden scream shattered the air.

"—*an ambush!*" hissed Espinosa.

Screams thundered in my ears. Savage screams of natives. Screams of dying men. My scalp prickled.

"All hands! All hands!" ordered Espinosa.

"Dear God," screamed the man with the swollen face. "They're killing them all!"

"Cut the anchor cables!" Espinosa cried. "Bring the ship in close!"

The deck of the *Trinidad* erupted with the few men left. We ran in confusion, some slashing the anchor cables, some raising sail, some loading the cannon, some falling to their knees. As I hacked at the anchor cable, sobbing, the wails of my shipmates filled my ears, "Dear God, help them! Serrano, the captains, the astrologer, the padre, so many! Dear God, dear God, dear God, *help us . . .*"

"Fire a broadside into the city!"

Cannon roared and the deck beneath my feet shuddered.

The air filled with black, rolling smoke and the acrid stench of gunpowder.

The beach swarmed with chaos. Through the smoke I saw one of our men stumble toward the ships, shouting something. A native shoved him from behind. He staggered and then dropped to his knees in the sand.

"Cease fire!" ordered Espinosa.

It was Captain Serrano. He was stripped and bleeding, his hands tied behind his back. Behind him stood the natives.

Then, as the smoke cleared, I saw what I had not seen before. Enrique.

He stood among the natives, unhurt.

Captain Serrano said, "They are dead. All of them. All except the padre and that lying Enrique." The words spat from his mouth. "Their throats have been cut. We have been betrayed."

"Betrayed? Why? Why would Enrique do such a thing? Why would Humabon?" Carvalho spoke from aboard the *Victoria,* which had drawn alongside us. I realized that besides Serrano, Carvalho was now the senior officer of the fleet.

"They say our Christian god is worthless. They say he did not save Magallanes and he will not save us now." A native kicked Serrano in the jaw and he fell to the sand.

I crossed myself.

Enrique stepped forward. "For the release of Serrano, Humabon demands two artillery pieces."

"Traitor!" screamed Carvalho.

Enrique's eyes narrowed. He shrieked his words, his voice shrill. "You dare call me a traitor? Who was it who refused to fight alongside my master? Who was it who watched from the safety of their vessels while my master was slain? Who ignored the will of my master, treating me like a dog? You are all traitors!"

"No, Carvalho." Serrano struggled to sit up in the sand. Blood trickled from his mouth. "Do not pay their ransom. They plan to seize whoever brings the ransom ashore. Again it is a trap." Several natives fell upon him, beating him with their fists, kicking his ribs. "Go!" he cried. "Leave me! There is nothing you can do! Better I should die than the whole fleet perish! As senior officer, I order you to depart at once!"

Like a drowning man gasping for breath before sinking beneath the waves, Serrano shouted his words to us, then disappeared under the flailing fists.

XXIII
May 1–28, 1521

Madness.

Utter madness.

We wandered—lost, alone, grieving—among many islands. Hundreds of them. Thousands, perhaps. Their beaches the same. Their trees the same. Some deserted. Some inhabited. Always we asked, Which way to the Spice Islands? Without Enrique, they could not understand us. We could not understand them.

Madness.

We beached and unloaded the *Concepción* and then set her afire. Men who had been her crew, who had tended her as if she were a lover, cried openly, weeping to see her timbers devoured by flame. Of the two hundred seventy-seven men who had embarked from Spain so long ago, only one hundred eight remained—a scant crew, enough to man but two vessels.

It is the way of the sea . . .

Espinosa was captain of the *Victoria*. Carvalho, as senior officer, was captain-general of the fleet and now captain of the *Trinidad.*

Already we hated Carvalho.

We hated his pointed nose, his pointed eyebrows, his thin lips. We hated his laugh; he laughed like a dog barks. We hated the fact that he drank rice wine at all hours. We hated him because he had turned coward and left Captain Serrano to his fate, a man who had been loyal to Magallanes from the beginning. We hated Carvalho because he had not even attempted a rescue, had not blown the natives to bits with our cannon. We hated him because he knew not where he was going and so blundered from island to island like a man gone blind. Most of all, we hated him because he was not Magallanes.

Such madness. All of us, mad.

Carvalho ordered us to capture and loot all vessels, as if we were pirates, as if we had never served under such a noble man as Magallanes. Angry, under orders, we attacked junks and captured the people aboard. We kept their goods, always asking, Which way to the Spice Islands?

I lived a personal nightmare of madness as well, forced to live my life whether I willed it or not. I moved my arms, my legs, breathed, sat, ate, as though watching myself from a distance. My mouth flapped like a puppet's, speaking words that came from far away. And whenever I slept, I awoke thrashing, my chest heaving, dripping with sweat. *There were too many, Rodrigo, too many. Forgive me, brother. I should never have let you go.*

Once we captured a native who painted my face with strange markings. The man pricked my cheek with a clawlike thorn. Then, using tiny, skilled stitches, he pulled soot-coated thread through my skin with a needle. After a few swirls on my cheekbone, I paid him in trinkets. The next day my face reddened and swelled. At first, my shipmates laughed and called me a fool. But after a week, my swellings disappeared and my scabbings healed and fell. Then they admired my design, saying that, along with my wild hair, it made me look savage and fearsome.

Curious to see what I looked like, I crept into what had been Magallanes's cabin. Carvalho lay asleep, his mouth open in a heavy, drunken snore. I peered at myself in the mirror and caught my breath. Indeed, I looked savage, as if I were some barbaric warrior, ferocious and battle-scarred. Slowly, I reached out a hand and touched the cool surface. I traced the face that stared back at me. Then, without warning, something inside of me burst open, horribly, viciously alive. And the face of the mighty warrior crumpled.

For you . . . Rodrigo . . . my brother.

So I will never forget.

One day we landed on a deserted beach to freshen our water casks. I was ordered by Carvalho to scrub his cask a second time since the stench hurt his nose.

"Again," he commanded.

Scarce able to hide my disgust at this weasel of a man, I scrubbed the cask again, my arms weary and aching, my knuckles scraped raw. I was covered with sweat and the sun dipped low in the sky by the time I finished. I was the last. My stomach growled angrily as the smell of roasted wild boar wafted toward me on the breeze. I heard the clunk of wooden dishes and the murmurs of my shipmates as they ate.

Before I could fill the cask with fresh water from the island's stream, a shadow stood over me. I glanced up to see Carvalho silhouetted in the orange of the setting sun. He leaned over my cask and sniffed. "Again, Cabin Boy."

I kicked the cask to the sand, shoved my face into Carvalho's, and snarled, "Go to hell, Captain-General."

I could feel his shock. The same shock hammered me. Already Carvalho was drawing his sword, his face blackened with fury.

Immediately I turned on my heels and fled into the jungle, whipping away vines and leaves, stumbling over roots, leaping over brush, my heart thundering. I ran and I ran, not knowing where, knowing only that if I did not run, I was dead. If Carvalho did not kill me himself, he would order my execution.

I sobbed as I ran. Choking. Already feeling the iron of the garrote as it tightened about my neck.

Before long, the darkness of the jungle closed around me. When I finally tripped over a root and sprawled on my face, I lay where I had fallen, exhausted, alone. I was far enough away. They would not find me until morning.

Things slithered around me, hissing, breathing.

I shivered. I had no shirt, no shoes. I wrapped my arms about me, but it did nothing to ease my shivering. Finally I buried myself in a pile of dead leaves. It did not last long. I soon jumped to my feet, cursing, brushing at myself furiously, for crawling things covered me.

I climbed a tree and sat in a crook of a branch, leaning back against the gnarled trunk, wondering how long a man can live with shame. Memories of the native burial ground returned. Never again, I decided, will I run. I shall retrace my steps. I shall turn myself in. Suffer my fate. I am not a coward.

I am Mateo Macías. Warrior. Man of courage.

So decided, I buried my face in my arms and slept a fitful sleep.

In the morning I returned to the beach, marching with my head high, my ears pounding with the rush of blood. The beach was empty, the waters deserted.

The ships were gone.

I sat beneath a palm tree and cursed my life.

Again I was alone. As in Ávila when my parents died of the pestilence. Ah, I reminded myself. You were not alone. You had Ugly. Here, you have nothing. Nothing.

I railed at my misfortune, that I would never see Spain again, that I would perish upon this island with no one to bury me, my flesh to become carrion, my bones to bleach. Marooned. Like Cartagena. For how many years must I endure this punishment? Five? Fifty? I toyed with my dagger, wondering if I should end my life. But I could not. It was a coward's way out. Besides, I thought, I want to live. Am I a coward for wanting to live?

That night, I dreamed that cannibals captured me and hung me from a tree, alive, like meat waiting for the butcher. They danced around me. As their hunger overtook them, they sliced a chunk from me and ate it raw, grinning, watching to see what I would do. They withdrew my innards, one at a time, sucking them from me like noodles until I was empty inside.

I awoke, my screams echoing through the hills.

When the sun rose, I wandered in search of food. Turtles' eggs, fallen coconuts, yellow figs, anything. I did not wander far, for now I was wary of cannibals, my skin crawling to think of them. I glanced into the jungle again and again, imagining fearsome faces smeared with war paint, a spear hurtling out of nowhere, a thousand screams.

About one hundred paces from the palm, I found a cross constructed of sticks. Had someone died? There was no inscription. Hesitating only a moment, I dug in the sand beneath the cross, wondering if I would brush the face of a dead shipmate with my fingers. Instead, I found a jug. Inside the jug, a message.

Behind the fallen tree you shall find supplies. Despair not. Despite Carvalho, we shall return. – Espinosa

A whirlwind of thoughts tumbled through me. They promise to return. When? Today? Tomorrow? And why? To kill me? To put me on trial and pronounce judgment? Nay, Espinosa would not leave me supplies and tell me not to despair if he planned only to turn the screws of the garrote. Besides, why would the fleet spend the effort to return if they only wanted me dead? For to leave me here is certain death. And what about Carvalho? How will they convince him to return? Will they be able to find the island again? One of many?

I pondered these questions while I sorted through the supplies. There was plenty of food, clothing, weapons, armor, tools, plus my guitar and artist's supplies. My heart suddenly overwhelmed me. I fell to my knees and wept.

XXIV
May 29–August 27, 1521

The next day I marched along the beach in full armor. Visor closed. Pike held high. Sword clanking at my side. Crossbow at the ready.

My steps sank deep into the sand.

The sun blazed.

It was my plan to perform a reconnaissance of the island, to map its shape and size and the location of landmarks and to discover if there were any native villages or cannibals. Then when the fleet returned in a few days, I would give a full report.

After several hundred paces, I opened my visor, panting, my armor already an oven.

Birds wheeled above me, cawing. Sand crabs skittered into the surf.

My armor became heavy. Each step was like moving a boulder. My ears filled with the sounds of my breathing and the creak of steel.

I paused to drink from a goatskin I had slung across my shoulder. Sweat ran in streams from my temples. Moisture drenched the clothing beneath my armor and it stuck to me like a second layer of skin. I left my sword and sword belt beneath a palm tree, thinking, I will return for it tomorrow. It is too loud. It warns of my approach.

For the next few hours, I skirted the eastern edge of the island, passing around a small cove, wishing I had brought more water. The island was bigger than I had realized. There was no other fresh water besides the stream back at camp. By now the sun was directly overhead.

On I marched, glancing into the jungle, my finger on the trigger of my crossbow. So far, there were no signs of natives. Usually villages were built close to the shore, close to fresh water. Regardless, I was ready. They would not catch me unawares. They would not cook me in their stew pot.

I stepped over a fallen tree and stumbled, crashing headlong, the sound thunderous in my ears. My crossbow fired into the sand with a twang. I lay there, cursing, thinking, If cannibals attack now, I am dead. When nothing happened, I heaved myself to my feet and continued, step by step, panting.

Several hours later, having finally left my leg armor behind, I reached the northern edge of the island, where the jungle closed with the beach. The trees loomed overhead, dark and eerily quiet. I did not like this side of the island and wished I had kept my sword. It was impossible to have too many weapons.

Suddenly something shrieked. The branches above my head rustled loudly. My heart lurched, and I raised my crossbow and fired as I yelled, knowing at the same time it was only a monkey. With a tumble and a crash, it landed at my feet, an arrow sticking from its throat. For a moment, a horrible moment, I was reminded of Rodrigo.

Now there were shrieks all around me, like demons howling.

"You will not get me," I screamed, shaking my fist at them. "I am Mateo Macías, warrior, man of courage!"

My words sounded foolish, even to me. I was screaming at monkeys.

I reloaded my crossbow and continued down the beach. One step, then another, finally leaving my helmet behind. I was sick of breathing my own breath and sniffing the stink of my body. Besides, I thought, I must listen alertly for any signs of attack. It is impossible to do that while the sounds of armor clank in my ears.

When finally darkness fell, I was forced to stop for the night. I sat with my back against a fallen tree, listening to my stomach complain, crossbow at the ready, pike at my side. Exhausted as I was, I did not sleep, seeing cannibals in every darkened shape, hearing them in every distant shriek. In the pale light of morning, I marched on, weak from hunger, parched with thirst. By the time I remembered my pike, still lying on the sand beside the fallen tree, I was too tired to return and fetch it.

When the sun finally rose from behind the island's peaks—twin mountains that rose from its center—I reached the western coast. Smaller hills surrounded the mountains, like piglets around a sow. Pig Island, I decided to call it. I now knew the island was about three leagues long, shaped like a bean, and inhabited by wild boars, monkeys, and a small spotted cat I had glimpsed watching me from its crook in a branch.

It was late afternoon when I finally staggered into camp. I flung off my breastplate. I cast aside my crossbow and devoured a supper of raw turtles' eggs.

Then, using seashells instead of beads, I prayed the rosary and afterward asked God to hurry the fleet to my rescue.

That night, I did not dream of cannibals.

Each day, each hour almost, I scanned the horizon. But always, always, it remained empty.

Meanwhile, I built a lean-to shelter of palm fronds where I slept the night and spent the hottest part of the day. In another lean-to close by, I stored my supplies. Occasionally crabs scuttled through my shelter. They were easy to catch. Lighting a fire not far away, I boiled the crabs in water from the stream. It was a good arrangement.

My lean-to worked well until one day in early summer when a nasty storm flattened my shelter and scattered my supplies. Standing amid the ruins, drenched to the skin, I realized blankly that I was now sixteen years old. That I had been so for almost one month but had forgotten. It took the next five days to rebuild my shelter, cutting stronger poles and strengthening it with vines found deep in the jungle.

My days were spent gathering fruit and stalking prey, preparing and cooking food, and looking after my shelter and supplies. It was familiar work.

My hair grew long, and I no longer bothered to shave.

At times I talked to myself, a yammering, ceaseless talk because I craved the sound of my own voice. Anxious for company, I would sometimes prepare another meal for Rodrigo or Magallanes. A palm frond for a plate. A pronged stick for a fork. A coconut shell for a bowl. And we would talk, Rodrigo and I, Magallanes and I, talk into the night, until I would fall upon the palm frond, weeping because, again, they had eaten nothing.

At other times, I lapsed into days of silence, my heart aching, my eyes weary from searching, always searching. Was this to be my life? Alone? Forever? Only pretending to have company? I asked myself these questions every day, every hour, every breath, sometimes wishing I had died alongside Rodrigo. Anything but this.

On one of these days of silence, I sank to the sand. "My Lord God," I prayed, "I can stand it no more. I am as one dead. Do not leave me here alone. Please." As I uttered the last word, a breeze filtered off the water, a cool breeze that kissed my face. My heart felt suddenly comforted, and for the first time since the death of my parents, peace flooded every fiber of my body. Perhaps, I thought, perhaps this is prayer. And I allowed the peace to wash over me as gently as the sea caresses the shore.

The sapling was about two and a half times my height and strong. I grasped its middle and bent its top down to the ground, let go, and watched it whip upright. "The Virgin Mary couldn't have picked a better one," I said aloud.

Several days before, I had eaten the last of the food supplies left me by my shipmates. Now I lived completely off the food of the island, which was proving harder than it at first had seemed—at least if I wanted to eat more than coconuts and crabs. Today I had decided to try something new. I would set a baited snare. I began to hack the branches from the tree with a hatchet. "But you see, my friend," I told myself, "the Virgin Mary wouldn't be in the jungle picking out saplings. She is much too busy. Besides, she would get covered with sap and might chop her thumb off. Still, maybe she needs a change of scenery besides the stable. Of course, she doesn't live in the stable anymore, everyone knows that; she lives in heaven. So why would she want to come here and pick out saplings when she can live in heaven? Ah . . . heaven. The food there must be delicious. I wonder, Rodrigo. Is the food in heaven delicious?"

Finished with stripping the branches off the sapling, I found a mature tree and chopped off a fresh branch as thick around as my wrist. I whittled one of its ends into a point. "Perhaps I will catch a wild boar . . . or a monkey . . . no, probably a lizard." I chopped off its other end so that it was only as long as my arm. A handsbreadth from the blunt end, I cut a deep notch. Then, two paces from the base of the sapling, I hammered the stake into the ground using a coconut. "Now ask yourself this, Mateo, if you eat all the turtles' eggs on the island, plus a turtle every once in a while, then someday won't all the turtles be gone?" I thought about this. It seemed a good question. Meanwhile I chopped a shorter length off the leftover branch, whittling a notch in it as well. "Well, everyone knows turtles live a long time . . . even without food and water, although what that has to do with anything, I don't know. Anyway, if they live a long time, and I'm only here a short time, then it shouldn't make any difference, should it? After I am gone, they will make more eggs."

Again bending the sapling down, I tied a short rope around its top. Keeping the tension, I tied the other end of the rope to the unnotched end of my newly whittled stake. I then slipped the new stake upside down into the grounded stake, notch pulling against notch. If all went well, when I released the sapling, it would stay bent. Slowly, carefully, I released the sapling. There was a momentary quivering. A groan. A creak of green wood. The stake in the ground shifted slightly, being pulled from above with all the sapling's might. I released my breath when everything held. Now to set my snare. "Well, truthfully, you are devouring an entire generation of turtles. Someday there will be only very, very old turtles. Still, unless you're here for eighty years—"

Before I could utter my next word, the stake yanked from the ground and the sapling whipped up, catching me full on the underside of my chin, snapping my jaws together and throwing me backward onto the jungle floor. I lay stunned, staring stupidly at the trees high overhead and the patterns they made against the sunlight. Already I could feel a giant welt rising. I tasted blood on my tongue. I blinked tears away.

Eighty years . . . is it truly so?

Eighty years . . .

I dragged myself to my feet, ignoring the sting. "Seems like you didn't pound in the stake deep enough, my friend." And I picked up the coconut to start again.

Three tries later, the stake held. Now, though, I was wise enough to move out of the way while testing its holding power. Next I set about making a snare. I made a small loop in one end of a short rope and threaded the other end of the rope through the loop to make a self-tightening noose. But when I went to attach the end of the rope to the upper stake, I realized that I would have to dismantle my setup, for the slightest amount of wiggling or tugging on the upper stake would immediately dislodge it from the grounded stake, causing the sapling to fling upright. I stood with the noose in my hand, dumbfounded at my stupidity. "Well, my friend, it appears you will have to begin again."

With a sigh, I set to work, undoing the sapling and then tying the end of the snare to the second stake. "On deck, on deck, gentlemen of the starboard watch, hurry up on deck, Mr. Pilot's watch, right now; get up, get up, get up!" After singing my little cabin-boy ditty, plus a few chanteys, I was finally back to where I'd started—the end of the snare tied securely to the second stake, the sapling taut and bent, the noose ready and waiting. I covered the noose with jungle debris, careful not to move it, scarce daring to breathe. Then I put half a crab in the center of the noose and stood back to survey my work. "A fine job, my friend. A fine day and a fine job."

Over the next five days I made more traps, getting faster each time. I checked my traps morning and afternoon. Always they were empty. What had I done wrong? I varied my bait—yellow figs, turtles' eggs, a dead fish I'd found. Then one day I stumbled across a half-grown piglet, dead on the jungle floor. I took it back to camp, cooked and ate some of it, saving the rest for bait and setting aside every drop of grease. Day after day of undisturbed traps made me believe that the animals could smell me. Perhaps pig smell would be better. So every day after, I smeared boar's grease over my feet and hands before leaving to check my traps.

A week later, I stood beside one of my traps. Fresh animal droppings dotted the area. The bait was gone. The trap unsprung. Whatever it was, it had eaten my bait and escaped unharmed. All that work for nothing. Nothing. Suddenly, something inside of me boiled, and I screamed, "You had no right to eat my bait! No right to escape! Don't you know I'm hungry? Don't you know I live here, too?" With a howl of rage, I kicked the empty air, kicked a nearby bush, kicked the stakes, and . . . *thwack!* The sapling whipped up and slapped me again on the underside of my chin.

Again I lay on my back, stunned, staring at trees.

Again tears coursed, hot and wicked.

I lay there a long time—until the light began to fade. Then, slowly, I got to my feet, my toe sore from kicking the stake. Equally as slowly, I reset my trap and then made my way back to camp.

The next day I stood beside one of my traps, staring, my mouth open with surprise. A wild boar hung from the sapling, dead, the noose tight about her neck.

It was a victory as sweet as if won on the battlefield.

XXV

September 4–October 27, 1521

The coolness of the water wrapped around me, rinsing the sweat from my body. The water was clear, and opening my eyes underwater, I could see everything. Creatures whose names I did not know, who perhaps were unnamed, crawled and swam, crept and swayed with the currents.

Two days ago I had returned to the cove on the eastern side, where the sea animals grew in·abundance. Although I was not a swimmer, the cove was shallow, and I found I could easily hold my breath, duck down beneath the water, and gather a shirtful of shell-fish. They were everywhere. I plucked them off the ocean floor as easily as I plucked lemons from a tree. Colorful fish surrounded me—brilliant oranges, golden yellows, midnight blues—some of them nibbling at me to see if I was good to eat. It was like swimming in a rainbow. Whenever I moved, the rainbow moved with me.

I rinsed the shellfish in the stream. When night came, I threw my feast upon the fire.

I often lit a fire, spending hours gazing into its depths. On this night, under the canopy of stars, I watched as the shells opened, one by one, heated over a bed of coals. As I devoured my little feast, dipping each morsel into melted boar's fat, I suddenly realized there was a different kind of courage. It was not the courage of facing my enemy in battle, girded to the teeth in armor, or the courage of returning to my own execution with my head held high. Instead, it was the courage to be alone day after day, not knowing what lay ahead, whether I would ever be rescued, whether I would live to hear the sound of another human voice.

It was the courage of endurance.

I wiped my hands and face on my shirt and poked a stick into the fire, thinking of Magallanes and the courage it took for him to endure. To move onward despite the mumbling of the crew, despite the many mutinies, despite the danger. I doubted I could have withstood such opposition. I doubted I could have endured such disapproval.

It was not that the captain-general had been perfect. He was a man only—like my father—perhaps even tinged with madness toward the end, who could say. But he was a man in whose memory I saw only courage and honor.

Then I remembered something Espinosa had said to Rodrigo long ago, something I think Rodrigo had finally understood before his death. *True honor is not purchased, but born. . . . It is honor within yourself.*

I stirred the fire with the stick, sending sparks into the night air, toward the stars. I withdrew the stick and gently blew on the tip, watching as it glowed orange.

Honor within.

Courage unseen.

Are they the same?

* * *

The next day, I built a memorial for Rodrigo. It had been preying on my mind for months, something unfinished. It was time.

I felled two small trees. After shaving off their branches and bark and trimming their ends, I lashed the smaller log to the larger log with vines to create a cross. On the cross beam I carved

RODRIGO NIETO DE CASTILE

DIED IN BATTLE APRIL 27, 1521

A BRAVE MAN

I heaved the cross over my shoulder and dragged it up a high hill. By the time I reached the top, sweat dripped from my body and I shook with fatigue. I set the cross down and, after fetching a shovel and a drink of water back at camp, began to dig a hole. When the hole was deep enough, I thrust the cross into the bottom. I worked most of the afternoon until it was secure, certain it could withstand the most powerful of winds.

Even in the ground, it stood one and a half times my height.

I knelt before the cross, feeling a hush come over my soul as my knees kissed the earth.

Rodrigo. My friend. My blood brother . . .

I promise you, should I ever get off this island, all of Spain shall know of your sacrifice, for I shall tell them of you, even if the king himself should ask me. How you stood beside our beloved captain-general and protected him with your life while others fled in terror.

Rodrigo, my brother, there is no greater honor.

Rest in peace, my friend.

The day swelled with heat and prickled with insects. Shirtless, barefoot, with a bandanna tied about my head, I stalked a spotted cat, my javelin hefted above my shoulder. I had long ago run out of crossbow bolts.

Spotted cats were difficult to stalk and even more difficult to kill. Their hearing and reflexes were sharper than mine, and it was only by surprise, by cunning, that I had ever caught one. But today I could not find a boar, my traps were empty, and the monkeys avoided me—flying through the treetops faster than I could run. The shellfish had all but disappeared in the shallow waters. Now if I wanted shellfish, I must learn to swim. And I sickened of fruit, crabs, and turtles' eggs.

As yet the cat had not detected me. She sprawled upon the limb of a giant tree, licking her paws. I crept silently, slowly. Leaves brushed my face as I passed, smelling of dampness. Vines dangled like snakes. I accidentally touched one and immediately the cat's head snapped in my direction. I froze. Yellow eyes watched while the vine swayed. When finally the vine stopped, the eyes blinked and the cat returned to her grooming.

Again I pressed forward.

Four paces. Five. Each one taking much time. Each footstep sinking into the soft, dark earth. Silent. I drew abreast of her, about fifteen paces away, and took aim. I would have one chance only.

The cat paused. She rotated her head toward me, yellow eyes alert, while I willed my muscles not to move, while I refused to blink, scarce daring to breathe. When she again looked away, I drew back the javelin and threw with all my might.

The javelin soared harmlessly over her back while she sprang from the tree and disappeared. I had no time to curse my poor aim, for at that very moment, the bushes to my left exploded with a gruntlike squeal and a flash of tusk. I fell hard on my back, the air slamming from my lungs. Burning pain sliced up my right leg, white-hot.

I screamed.

Again it attacked.

My dagger was suddenly in my hands, and I was stabbing wildly. Screaming as I lay on my back. Blood spattering my face, my eyes, my mouth.

Then my head shattered with pain and I knew no more.

The cry of a parrot awakened me, and I sat up with a start. Immediately I lay back again, groaning, my head pounding. What happened? Where am I? Slowly the memory returned. An attack by a wild boar. He had gored me, this I knew. How badly, I knew not. Despite the pain, I forced my eyes open. It was early morning. I had lain senseless for half a day and a night.

I raised myself to my elbow. Pain washed through my head, vibrant and vicious. Beside me lay the boar, a dagger protruding from his ribs. Ants crawled over him in black rivers.

The inner thigh of my right leg had been pierced. Wincing, I probed the wound. For such a deep wound, it had not bled much. But my head . . . ah, my head! My fingers felt a huge, swollen gash along my left temple. I was sticky with blood, my bandanna stiff. The same ants that crawled on the boar crawled on me. I spat them out of my mouth but had not the strength to brush them off.

I must return to camp, I thought. To draw water and bathe. To cleanse and bandage my wounds. And I am thirsty. So thirsty. I stood, clenching my teeth, battling the waves of sickness. It was too much. I leaned over and vomited, fighting the darkness that threatened to suck me down.

Afterward, unsteady and shaking, I withdrew my dagger from the boar and stuck it in my sheath. I would clean it later. At first I dragged the carcass, unwilling to leave such prized meat behind. But I was a league from camp, and after twenty paces or so, I knew I would have to retrieve him later. It would take all my strength to return alone.

The sun was setting when I finally staggered into camp. I gulped water from the stream, stumbled to my shelter, and collapsed. I was quickly asleep.

Fog crept through the depths of my mind. Sometimes an icy mist, slithering, sometimes blasting with heat, smoke from a red-hot forge. I tried to wake but could not. Then the effort of waking grew too tiring, and I released myself to the fog. It deepened . . . swirling . . . deadly. . . .

Awakening with a start, I sat bolt upright, gasping. My heart thundered in my ears. I could not catch my breath, and my body felt afire. Again it was day.

I am sick, I thought with alarm.

I dragged myself to the stream and drank deeply. It was all I could do. Beside the stream—half in, half out of the water—I slept again, my mind drunken with haze. . . .

My father stands in the doorway of our house. Although the shadows hide his face, I know he is looking at me. I yearn to go to him but cannot move. I yearn to ask him why he's been gone so long, but my mouth won't open and my tongue feels wooden. Instead I lay on my back in the courtyard. The sun beats on me, and I stare at him helplessly.

Then I see tongues of flame. They dance behind him and lick his hair. He laughs, unhurt.

Never have I heard my father laugh.

Now the flames surround him, but he parts them like a curtain and, still laughing, strides easily into the courtyard to stand beside me. The flames disappear, and where they once were grows a beautiful garden. A sweet fragrance reaches me. His hands touch my face and his touch is cool, like balm. "My son," he says. "It is time for you to go home. Go home, my son. Go."

Shapes and shadows invaded my fog. Voices from a thousand dreams. They surrounded me. Stripped the clothes from my body. Washed me. Carried me. Many hands.

XXVI
November 1–December 21, 1521

I awakened to darkness.

A swaying, creaking darkness that stank of rot. A pounding above my head, like feet upon a deck. Water sloshing, as if against the hull of a ship.

I lay there, unbelieving. The dream continues, I thought. I still sleep. I have dreamed this dream many times.

Then in the dream appeared a light. The light swayed, as though someone approached holding a lantern.

A face.

"Espinosa?" I asked. My voice, cracked and feeble, sounded so real, so loud in my ears.

Setting the lantern aside, the man knelt next to me where I lay on a pallet. "You are awake," he said.

I gaped at him. "Is it really you?"

He laughed and grasped my hand, his grip as I had always remembered it, a grip like iron. "Aye, Mateo. It is good to see you again. We thought you were lost to us. You have been senseless for some five days now."

My throat clogged, a lump forming in place of words. Finally, after all the months of solitude, after all the questions that had burned on my lips, aching for release, all I could say was, "I thought you'd left me forever."

Espinosa sighed. "Aye. We were lost. We could no more find your island than we could find the Spice Islands."

"But Carvalho—"

"—has been deposed."

"Deposed?" I sat up, gritting my teeth against the dizziness.

"He was an incompetent leader. Drunk most of the time. The final straw was when he forced captive women into his cabin."

"You mutinied?"

"Nay, Mateo. I am sick of betrayal. We all are. Instead we gathered on an island, beneath the palms, and voted him out. We elected a new captain-general."

"You?"

He nodded. "I am now captain-general and captain of the *Trinidad,* and Cano, one of the mutineers at Port San Julián, is captain of the *Victoria.* We have done what Carvalho could not."

"Which is?"

"We have found the Spice Islands. In a few days, if the winds favor us, we shall arrive." Espinosa clasped my hand again. From the expression on his face, I knew him to be pleased—as pleased and happy as I had ever seen him.

I spent the evening on deck, surrounded by shipmates who clapped me on the back, who gave me extra portions of their food and drink until my stomach tightened like a drum. I know I had a silly grin pasted on my face, but I could not help it, nor did I care. I was home. *Home*. I could not stop looking at them. Each face, once lost forever, now so precious. My friends. My brothers.

On the eighth day of November, we dropped anchor at the Spice Islands. It was another tropical paradise of gleaming sands, broken shells washed bone white, and swollen, lush mountains that smelled of jungle.

Someone told me that the mountains were covered with a perpetual mist, that a cloud descended every day without fail, that the mist provided the proper moisture for the growing of cloves, and that nowhere else in the world could cloves be grown. Three days after our arrival, while the leaves of the jungle steamed after a morning's pounding deluge, I wandered into the mountains to sketch the cloves. Though plagued with a headache, I was well enough now to carry out my duties as the fleet artist.

I tramped through the mists and studied the trees. The trees grew tall, their trunks as big around as I was, the cloves growing in clusters at the tips of the branches. I drew until the light began to fade.

On another excursion, a companion and I found nutmeg trees, which resembled walnut trees, with the same leaf, their fruit like an apricot. I split one of the fruit in two, exposing a crimson-colored casing, which my companion said was the source of mace. The casing surrounded a single brown seed, the nutmeg. I held the nutmeg in my hand, amazed that so many lives had been lost over a simple nut.

From the moment of our arrival, we had been welcomed by the natives. The rajah of the Spice Islands came aboard the *Trinidad*.

"I dreamed ships came to the Spice Islands from a faraway land," he said as he held out his hand to be kissed. "When I awakened from my dream, I looked to the moon, desiring to know the truth. And in the moon's face I saw you coming and knew you to be my friends. It is good you are Spaniards and not Portuguese, for the Portuguese have been difficult of late. I would be honored to have a treaty with Spain. You are now as sons to me. Go ashore as if you were home. From henceforth, this island shall be called Castile."

We set up a trading outpost. I purchased bags of nutmeg, ginger, pepper, cinnamon, and cloves. I would return to Spain a wealthy man, for what I could buy for a few coins here, I could sell in Spain for a hundred times its worth. I also took the money Rodrigo had earned selling rats, plus his gold nuggets from Cebu, and purchased spices. Someday I would find his family and give them spices. Spices instead of Rodrigo. A poor exchange.

Come December, we prepared for departure. We bent new sails to the yards, each sail a crisp white with the blue cross of Santiago upon its center and the words *ÈSTA ES LA ENSEÑA DE NEUSTRA BUENAVENTURA*, This is the sign of our good fortune. Finally, the last of the cloves was loaded.

On the eighteenth day of December, our holds bursting with spices, the ships' bellies low in the water, we prepared to set sail. The air buzzed with happy chatter, and we took off our caps and cheered when the master cried, "Prepare to up anchor for home!"

Everyone jumped to obey orders. Grins stretched from ear to ear. We were going home! After so many months away from Spain, after the loss of so many friends, certain none of us would make it back alive, finally, we were going *home*! We sang our chanteys lustily. Round the capstan. Astraddle the yards. The sigh of canvas and the thud of tackle. The steady stream of commands from the fo'c'sle, the quarterdeck, the main deck.

"Sheet home and hoist away topsails!"

Ahead of us, the *Victoria* left the harbor.

The *Trinidad* began to follow, slowly. Suddenly she groaned. "The anchor's snagged! The anchor's snagged!" cried one of the seaman. "It won't budge!"

For a moment, a breath only, every man on the *Trinidad* stood rooted. Above us the *Trinidad*'s topsails filled with wind. Beneath us, she strained against her anchor. An enormous shudder passed from stern to bow. Suddenly chaos erupted. Men dashed everywhere.

"Cut the anchor! Cut the anchor!"

"Let fly the sheets!"

But it was too late.

"She's too full!" shouted someone from the hatch. "The strain has split a seam in her timbers! Water is pouring into the bilge! We need men on the pumps! Fast!"

In an instant, it was over. Our voyage home was cut short by ill timing and poor luck. By the time the *Victoria* returned, curious why we had not followed, we had beached the *Trinidad* and heeled her over to stem the leak. As we unloaded her—spices, cannon, food, water casks—I could not bear to look at anyone.

Spain. Would I ever return?

Then Espinosa gathered both ships' crews together. As I stood among my shipmates, I could feel our heartbreak, our dream turned to nightmare. "The news is not good," he said. "The *Trinidad* will take months of repairs."

Behind me, I heard someone weeping.

Espinosa continued. "I have decided that the *Victoria* will sail for Spain. I will stay behind with the *Trinidad* and follow when we can. That is all. You are dismissed."

No one left. We stood, silent, absorbing the shock of this news, before a sailor spoke the thoughts that screamed through everyone's mind. "But, Captain Espinosa, how will we decide who leaves on the *Victoria* and who stays behind on the *Trinidad*? Everyone wants to return to Spain. Everyone wants to be aboard the *Victoria*."

Espinosa sighed heavily. "Very well. We shall draw lots."

An hour later, we gathered around Espinosa, each of us reaching into a bag he held. A blue crystal meant a sailor would leave aboard the *Victoria*. A green crystal meant a sailor would stay with the *Trinidad*.

It was my turn. I thrust my arm into the large bag and closed my eyes. I felt the differently shaped crystals. It was impossible to tell what color they were. My hands trembled as I went from crystal to crystal, praying God to guide me.

I grasped a crystal. This is the one, I thought. I withdrew it from the bag.

It was blue.

I was going home.

In a few days, the *Victoria* was again ready to sail. We waited until afternoon, for the men aboard the *Trinidad* would not let us leave until they had finished writing letters for home. My hand cramped with writing, for I was one of the few who could write. Not well, but it did not matter. One by one, they came to me.

214

Whispered sighs. . . .

Messages of love. . . .

Dried flowers pressed into my hand. . . .

But as my quill scratched over the paper, ten letters, twenty, my heart became a well of the blackest ink. I, who had no one, would soon return to Spain. Yet they, who had wives, children, mothers and fathers, sisters and brothers, would remain at the Spice Islands. Perhaps not returning home for another year or more, perhaps never returning home.

"Tell my—tell my wife I love her," said Espinosa in a voice as parched as the ground of Castile. "I know not the words to use. You fashion the words. Tell her someday I will return to her. Tell her nothing will keep me from returning home to Spain. Nothing." Espinosa continued, and when he finished, he placed his hand on my shoulder as I sealed his letter with melted wax. "Fare thee well, Mateo. You are a good lad. I have been proud to call you friend."

Words choked in my throat. Espinosa squeezed my shoulder one last time and was gone.

Finally at midday, with forty-seven crew, many spices, and an additional thirteen natives who had signed on as crew members, the *Victoria* weighed anchor. The *Trinidad*'s men followed in their ship's boats as we slipped away. They rowed frantically, their expressions desperate, filled with longing.

"Tell my wife I love her!"

"Tell my children I shall return home!"

"Give my family my spices! Tell them I will not be long in coming!"

Then, as one, they dropped the oars in the oarlocks and stood, shouting farewells. Their arms stretched toward us.

We rushed aft, weeping, hanging over the *Victoria's* stern, altogether almost two hundred arms stretching across the waters as if to embrace for the last time.

"I shall never forget you, my friends!" I cried. "We have been through much together! May God protect you!"

"Farewell!"

"Until we meet again, my brothers!"

"Godspeed!"

Gradually the gap between us widened. First a stream, then a river, then a great gulf. One by one, our voices trailed away until we stood silent, shoulder to shoulder, our arms hanging at our sides. The ship's boats grew smaller. Smaller. The *Trinidad,* too, dwindled . . . a dot only . . . until finally she vanished.

Still we did not move. *It should not have been this way,* I thought. *So many left behind. For you, my friends, for you will we make it home. For you will we survive. I promise.*

Suddenly, over our heads, the wind intensified. My cap blew from my head, tumbling against the bulwarks. Beside me the captain drew a deep breath, paused, and then barked, "Helm a-starboard!"

"Aye, aye, sir!" came the helmsman's cry.

The *Victoria* fell off to larboard. The masts and yards creaked. Water thwacked against the hull as she picked up speed.

"Helm amidships! Steady as she goes!"

I leaned over the stern. The wake frothed and bubbled. Wind whipped my hair, lashing my face. Tears streamed down my cheeks.

You were right, Rodrigo, my brother. You were right.

It is the way of the sea.

September 1522

On the sixth day of September, in the year of our Lord 1522, the *Victoria* hove to off the mouth of the Río Guadalquivir. Aboard we were twenty-one men. Eighteen men returning home and three natives. All that remained of two hundred seventy-seven men.

The voyage home, which we had thought would be swift, carefree almost, was as difficult as all that had come before. Why should we have believed it would be easy? Because the possibility of enduring more suffering was unthinkable. But again, unable to find food, ravaged by storms and rebuffed by contrary winds, many men had died, their fingers stretched toward home.

I saw the shocked looks on the faces of people as they rowed their boats out to greet us. Our ship was in tatters, her sails grayed and filthy, her hull thickened with barnacles, putrid with seaweed. And we, her crew, starved—at times so hungry we had eaten our spices. Our clothes hung in rags, our faces gaunt and white—the faces of skeletons.

We watched the boats approach.

"We are all that remains of the voyage of Magallanes!" cried our captain. "We sailed into the west and have returned from the east. We have been at sea three years less fourteen days. We have not the strength to tow ourselves upriver to Seville, and our longboat is gone."

Whispers spread among the people like fire. They gazed at us with astonishment. And in that moment I realized the magnitude of what we had accomplished. It was a monumental achievement, a deed that would surely be remembered throughout all of history.

A longboat crew was quickly arranged to tow the *Victoria* upriver. We would leave in the morning. Meanwhile, food and wine were brought aboard. We feasted, wetting our bread with tears that would not cease falling. And we were not ashamed.

Two days later we arrived in Seville, where we fired our cannon in honor of our fallen shipmates and in honor of our captain-general, Magallanes.

Through the streets we shuffled, gaunt as sticks, mere shadows of men. Each of us carried a burning candle. We passed through the narrow passageways, shadows leaping from wall to wall, and arrived at the shrine of Nuestra Señora de la Victoria. We knelt before the altar. It was a promise we had made long ago, should we survive.

I held the candle. *It is my reflection*, I thought. *And in its flame I can see myself. . . .*

I have been forged with fire.

I have held dying friends in my arms. I have tasted grief and betrayal, suffering and loneliness. And yet, I have known true honor, courage, love, and the joy of brotherhood.

I knew not what my future held, only knowing that it opened before me like blossoms of fragrant, exotic flowers, that it burned as brightly as the candle in my hands. And I thanked God for the day a master-at-arms befriended a poor shepherd's son who sang unnoticed in a dirty, noisy inn.

After much time, I rose to my feet, stiffened, aware of the clamor outside. I set my candle on the altar and left the shrine.

Crowds swarmed around me. I could scarce move, so great was the commotion. We were famous, invited to the king's court, but I no longer cared for such things. I moved through the crowd, trying to shake them from me. Many strangers sought to touch me.

And then I saw him.

An ugly dog.

Spotted with mange, the dog lounged in the shadow of a nearby building, panting, his tongue lolling out of his mouth. Could it be? I stared for a moment, disbelieving, then motioned to him. He came immediately, sat on his haunches before me.

I knelt, wrapped my arms about him, and buried my face in his neck.

AFTERWORD

Except for Mateo, his parents, Aysó, and the people at the inn, all the characters in *To the Edge of the World* really existed. Even Rodrigo! Rodrigo Nieto was a servant for Cartagena aboard the *San Antonio* who later transferred to the *Trinidad*. Rodrigo was killed at the Battle of Mactan while defending Magellan. Another man who defended Magellan was Antonio Pigafetta. It was he who "suffered from the bite of a poisoned arrow, his face so swollen he could not open his eyes." Fortunately for history, Pigafetta not only survived the voyage but also kept a journal. Many of his vivid descriptions are woven throughout the story, such as the one of the guanaco—the wild ancestor of the llama— having "the neck and body of a camel, the head and ears of a mule, and the tail of a horse." Portions of the dialogue between Magellan and Cartagena were taken from eyewitness accounts.

Some have asked why the name Magallanes was used instead of Magellan. Ferdinand Magellan is the English translation of his Portuguese name, Fernão de Magalhães. However, I felt his native Portuguese tongue to be too intimidating for Western readers. Instead, I settled upon the Spanish translation, Fernando de Magallanes (the *g* is silent, sounding like an *h*), to give the novel added Spanish flavor, and in deference to our young Spanish narrator.

While the events in *To the Edge of the World* are faithful to history, even so, it is important to understand that there are limited accounts available of the actual voyage. Most are contradictory and have a political agenda. Also, for the sake of economy, some of the voyage's elements were abridged or omitted, since recounting the voyage in every detail was beyond the scope of this novel. In addition, whenever a historical event is recounted by a fictional character, the character will always color the story with his or her experiences, interactions, and interpretations.

During this period in history, values were in many instances very different from those we hold today, and punishments extreme. For example, like his contemporaries, Mateo considered anyone from a less advanced culture to be a "savage," uncivilized by European standards. In capturing the two Patagonian natives, for instance, the Europeans probably believed they were doing the natives a favor. After all, in the eyes of the crew, the "savages" were just half-naked people, unfortunate enough to live in a frozen, bleak environment. Magellan could clothe them, teach them to speak properly, baptize them into Christianity, and introduce them to Europe. It would never have occurred to someone in that day that kidnapping a native was wrong. It is only now, looking back upon history, that we can see the wrong so clearly. Even Mateo did not think it was wrong.

It is also troubling for people of the twenty-first century to read about the forced religious conversions of native peoples by Magellan. But to understand Magellan, it is necessary to know the historical backdrop in which he operated. Magellan's concept of religion was in great part a product of his time. For Christians, it was a time of religious intolerance, when it was believed that history would end and Christ would return only when all the world had converted to Christianity, namely Catholicism. (Within this theology lay huge economic advantage as well, as conversion to Catholicism usually coincided with trade treaties and economic loyalty to the sovereign state, and refusal to convert led to mass destruction and confiscation of all worldly possessions.) Under such a belief, the end justified the means, and all acts to bring about its fulfillment became "holy," regardless of their morality. Crusaders were seen as devout soldiers for Christ, armed to defend Christendom against infidels and to conquer lands in the name of Christ. Spain saw herself as the champion of Christianity and instituted the Inquisition to establish religious unity. This unity was accomplished through the capture, torture, and trial of heretics, resulting in the deaths of thousands—Jews, Moors, Protestants—anyone who refused the Catholic faith. As an inheritor of this religious environment, then, Magellan felt the baptism of native populations to be a crucial element in annexing a new land for Spain. Compared to later conquistadors such as Francisco Pizarro and Hernándo Cortés, who exhibited gruesome—but accepted—rapaciousness toward the natives of the New World, Magellan stands as a paragon of virtue, fiercely loyal to the island chiefs with whom he'd made treaties of peace.

Nowadays, it also is difficult to understand the Europeans' craze for spices. But in those days, there was no refrigeration. Pepper was essential in the preservation of foods and, pound for pound, was equal in value to gold. Spices also transformed a bland, tasteless diet into something palatable. Imagine eating food with no spices whatsoever! At that time, spices were available only from a certain part of the world—the Spice Islands, located in the Far East. Spices were transported overland from India to Europe, passing from one middleman to the next, ultimately selling for exorbitant prices.

After many failed attempts, a sea route to India was eventually established in 1497 by the Portuguese, via Africa's Cape of Good Hope. The Portuguese then wrested the affluent spice trade out of Muslim hands, something Spain observed with an envious eye. Because Portugal had earlier been granted a monopoly on trade routes to the east by the pope, Spain was forced to turn to the west in search of a trade route, sending out such men as Christopher Columbus in 1492 and Ferdinand Magellan in 1519.

Magellan's accomplishment in circumnavigating the globe cannot be overestimated. With the exception of the Vikings to the north, it wasn't until the mid-1400s that European ships were stout enough to venture onto the open ocean. Prior to that, they had been limited to the Mediterranean Sea. It wasn't until 1492 that the "southern continent" (South America) was discovered, and even then, the full scale of its enormousness was unknown. Likewise, in 1513, Europeans discovered the existence of the South Sea (Pacific Ocean), first viewed by Vasco Núñez de Balboa from the isthmus of Panama. Preservation of food for such extended voyages of exploration was not possible. Charts were inaccurate and incomplete. The vastness of the Pacific Ocean had been grossly underestimated. Longitude was impossible to calculate accurately and had to be estimated through "dead reckoning," a method in which a mariner "reckoned" his ship's speed by the use of a crude measuring device, enabling him to calculate how far he'd sailed. Over a three-year voyage, dead reckoning compounded error upon error. Above all, successful navigation of Magellan's ships through unknown, uncharted waters is nothing short of astounding. Even today, *el paso*—now known as the Strait of Magellan—is a maze of dead ends, dangerous currents, and contrary winds, a waterway avoided by all but the most experienced, or most foolish, of mariners.

Whatever happened to the largest ship of the fleet, the *San Antonio,* which vanished in the strait? Instead of exploring the strait as ordered, there was a mutiny aboard. The ship's pilot, Gómez, harbored a grudge against Magellan, having been turned down by the king for a similar expedition several years prior. Under Gómez's influence, the crew overpowered the *San Antonio*'s captain, a relative of Magellan's, and set a course for Spain. For unknown reasons, the *San Antonio* did not return to Port San Julián to fetch Cartagena. Cartagena was never heard from again.

Once the *San Antonio* arrived in Spain, Gómez testified against Magellan, listing many atrocities. In response to Gómez's testimony and in response to the marooning of Cartagena, government officials cast the captain of the *San Antonio* into prison and placed Magellan's wife and son under house arrest.

A more balanced truth was revealed, however, when the survivors of the *Victoria* returned home a year and a half later. They were called to testify regarding Gómez's allegations against Magellan. The survivors denied Gómez's charges, and the captain of the *San Antonio* was released from prison. It was too late for Magellan's wife and child, however, as they had died before the *Victoria*'s return.

What of the *Trinidad*'s crew? Following months of repairs, the *Trinidad* attempted to sail eastward across the Pacific Ocean. But repelled by the winds, after many months she arrived back where she started at the Spice Islands. This time, however, the Portuguese had assembled in force. They captured the crew of the *Trinidad* and imprisoned them in India. Of the *Trinidad*'s crew, only four lived to see Spain again. One of those four was Espinosa. Carvalho died of illness while the *Trinidad* was undergoing repairs.

As for the *Victoria,* she was lost with all hands in the mid-Atlantic on a subsequent voyage.

In terms of spices, of riches, the expedition failed. The strait was impossible to navigate. Later expeditions found it easier to go around the cape, not many leagues south. The westward route was too long, too tortuous, and the price in human lives too costly. All Spanish claims to the Spice Islands were sold to Portugal in 1529 for three hundred fifty thousand golden ducats. But in terms of human achievement, of exploration, Magellan's circumnavigation of the world remains unsurpassed.

GLOSSARY

aft - Toward the rear of the vessel.

armada - A fleet of ships.

astern - Behind the ship.

atoll - A ring-shaped coral reef or a string of closely spaced small coral islands.

ballast - Weight placed low inside a ship, necessary to balance the ship upon the waters.

Basque - A person from the Basque province in northern Spain.

bilge - An enclosed section at the bottom of the ship where seawater collects.

bow - The front of the ship.

bulkhead - A wall-like structure inside a ship.

bulwarks - The built-up sidewalls above the deck of a ship.

capstan - A barrel-like mechanism, designed for hauling in heavy loads such as an anchor. The capstan is rotated circularly by pushing long handles that extend like spokes out of the top of the capstan.

careen - To lay a ship on its side for repairs, caulking, and cleaning.

Castile - A former kingdom in central Spain covering most of its interior. *Castile* means "castle" in Spanish.

caulk - To plug the seams of a boat with oakum or other waterproof materials; to make the ship watertight.

chanteys - Songs sung by sailors while at work.

ducat - A gold coin, worth about forty-two U.S. dollars today.

ebb tide - The flowing of water back into the sea, resulting in a low tide onshore (the opposite of flood, which results in a high tide).

el paso - "The passage" in Spanish. Today this difficult passage through the South American continent is known as the Strait of Magellan.

flagrante delicto - In the very act of committing the offense.

fo'c'sle - (abbreviation and proper pronunciation for *forecastle*) The forward section of the ship, directly behind the bow and forward of the foremast. In the ships, these were raised decks, accessible by a companion-way or ladder. In later vessels, the crew's sleeping quarters were enclosed under the fo'c'sle.

gangplank - A movable platform that extends from the gangway of a ship to a dock, pier, or shore, used by the crew to embark and disembark.

gangway - The place at a ship's side where people embark and disembark.

garrote - A former method of execution in Spain. An iron collar was placed around the condemned person's neck and tightened by means of screws. Death occurred by strangulation.

gunwale - The upper edge of a ship's side.

halyards - The ropes and lines used to hoist sails, yards, flags, etc.

harquebus - A long gun, resembling a rifle, operating with a matchlock or wheel-lock mechanism. Developed in mid-fifteenth-century Spain, it preceded the musket.

hove to - The past tense of the verb phrase "heave to," meaning "to bring a ship to a stop."

hull - The main body of a ship.

islet - A very small island.

javelin - A lightweight spear.

junk - A square-rigged ship used mostly in the waters around China.

lance - A long wooden spear tipped with steel.

larboard - The left side of a vessel when facing forward. The term *larboard* was officially replaced by the current term *port* in 1844 to prevent confusion with *starboard*. The term was also used to designate one of the watches.

league - Three miles.

leeward - The side of the ship away from the direction of the wind (the opposite of windward). Fires were lit on the leeward (or lee) side to keep smoke and hot embers away from the sails and rigging.

longboat - The largest boat carried by a sailing ship; any of the various two-masted vessels used for sailing or rowing in coastal waters. About twenty-three feet long, it was towed behind the ship. A longboat could transport cannon, anchors, and many men.

mace - A spice consisting of the fibrous layer between the nutmeg's shell and husk. Mace has a fragrance like that of nutmeg and a slightly warm taste.

mange - A parasitic skin disease in animals characterized by loss of hair and scabby eruptions.

Mar Pacifico - The "Peaceful Sea" in Spanish. The first European to sight the Pacific Ocean was Vasco Núñiez de Balboa in 1513. At that time it was called Balboa's Sea or the South Sea. Magellan and his men were the first Europeans to sail upon its waters, and impressed by its calmness, Magellan named it the Pacific.

oakum - A fiber obtained by untwisting old ropes. Used in caulking a ship's timbers.

pace - The distance of a man's stride, approximately two and a half feet.

padre - "Priest" in Spanish.

palm - A unit of measure based on the width or length of the palm of the hand. When based on the width, the palm is between three and four inches. When based on the length, the palm is between seven and ten inches. Using the length of the palm as the calculation for the height of the giant native, he would have been anywhere between five feet ten inches and eight feet four inches tall.

pestilence - In past centuries it referred to the bubonic plague.

pike - A wooden spear tipped with steel.

pilot - The officer responsible for a ship's navigation.

plague - Scurvy. In sixteenth-century Europe, the names and causes of diseases were unknown. What we know today as scurvy was then only called the plague. (What we call today the bubonic plague was then called the pestilence.)

poop - A raised deck at the stern of a ship.

quarterdeck - The deck immediately below the stern deck, or sterncastle.

rajah - A chieftain or prince in India and areas of Southeast Asia.

real - (pronounced ray-AHL) A silver coin worth, at that time, about one-eighth of a U.S. dollar.

rigging - The lines and ropes of a vessel used to support the masts and work the yards and sails.

río - "River" in Spanish.

San Elmo - Saint Elmo, the patron saint of sailors. What the crews experienced was called Saint Elmo's fire. During an electrical storm, an electrical discharge glows from the tips of masts and the yardarms. To the sailors, it was a visible sign that Saint Elmo was watching over them.

Santiago - "Saint James" in Spanish.

scabbard - A sheath in which to store a sword.

scuppers - Openings cut through the bulwarks to drain seawater.

scurvy - A disease caused by vitamin C deficiency characterized by swelling and bleeding of the gums.

scuttle - To deliberately sink a ship.

Sed Preso - "You are under arrest" in Spanish.

shrouds - The lines and ropes that stretch from the top of the mast (the masthead) to the sides of the vessel to support the mast. Sailors climbed the shrouds if they needed to go aloft. The shrouds had horizontal rope rungs called ratlines (pronounced RAT-lins).

skiff - A boat small enough for sailing or rowing by one person.

starboard - The right side of a vessel when facing forward. Also the designation of one of the watches.

stern - The back of the ship.

sterncastle - (or aftercastle) Located at the stern of the ship and consisting of a raised deck under which was usually a cabin that housed the captain and sometimes other officers.

swivel gun - A mounted gun able to swivel and fire in any direction.

waist deck - The portion of decking in the waist, or center, of a vessel. In many ships this was open to the elements, enclosed on both fore and aft sides by raised decks.

wake - The swirling water that appears behind a moving vessel.

weevil - A type of beetle that feeds especially on grain, nuts, and fruit.

yard - The horizontal beam attached to the mast to support the sails.

yardarm - The end of the yard.

BIBLIOGRAPHY

Buehr, Walter. *Ships and Life Afloat: From Gallery to Turbine*. New York: Charles Scribner's Sons, 1953.

Cameron, Ian. *Magellan and the First Circumnavigation of the World*. New York: Saturday Review Press, 1973.

Crow, John A. *Spain: The Root and the Flower*. 3rd ed., expanded and updated. Berkeley and Los Angeles: University of California Press, 1985.

Culver, Henry B. *The Book of Old Ships*. New York: Bonanza Books, 1974.

Daniel, Hawthorne. *Ferdinand Magellan*. New York: Doubleday and Company, Inc., 1964.

Defourneaux, Marcelin. *Daily Life in Spain in the Golden Age*. Translated by Newton Branch. Stanford, California: Stanford University Press, 1966.

Fuentes, Carlos. *The Buried Mirror: Reflections on Spain and the New World*. New York, New York: Houghton Mifflin Company, 1992.

García, Cristina Rodero. *Festivals and Rituals of Spain*. New York: Harry N. Abrams, Inc., 1994.

Harland, John. *Seamanship in the Age of Sail: An Account of the Shiphandling of the Sailing Man-of-War 1600–1860, Based on Contemporary Sources*. Annapolis, Maryland: United States Naval Institute, 1984.

Hildebrand, Arthur Sturges. *Magellan*. New York: Harcourt, Brace and Company, 1924.

Humble, Richard. *The Explorers*. Alexandria, Virginia: Time-Life Books, 1978.

Joyner, Tim. *Magellan*. Camden, Maine: International Marine Publishing/ McGraw-Hill Books, 1992.

Kemp, Peter, ed. *The Oxford Companion to Ships and the Sea*. Oxford: Oxford University Press, 1976.

McBrien, Richard P. *Inside Catholicism: Rituals and Symbols Revealed.* Edited by Barbara Roether. San Francisco: Collins Publishers San Francisco, 1995.

Michener, James A. *Iberia: Spanish Travels and Reflections.* New York: Random House, Inc., 1968.

Nowell, Charles E., ed. *Magellan's Voyage Around the World: Three Contemporary Accounts: Antonio Pigafetta, Maximilian of Transylvania, and Gaspar Corrêa.* Evanston, Illinois: Northwestern University Press, 1962.

Ober, Frederick A. *Ferdinand Magellan.* Heroes of American History. New York: Harper and Brothers Publishers, 1907.

Parr, Charles McKew. *So Noble a Captain: The Life and Times of Ferdinand Magellan.* New York: Thomas Y. Crowell Company, 1953.

Parry, J. H. *Romance of the Sea.* Washington, D.C.: National Geographic Society, 1981.

Pastor, Xavier. *Anatomy of the Ship: The Ships of Christopher Columbus.* Annapolis, Maryland: Naval Institute Press, 1992.

Pigafetta, Antonio. *The Voyage of Magellan.* Translated by Paula Spurlin Paige from the edition in the William L. Clements Library. Englewood Cliffs, New Jersey: Prentice-Hall, Inc., 1969.

Silverberg, Robert. *The Longest Voyage.* New York: Bobbs-Merrill Company, Inc., 1972.

Simmons, Marc, Donna Pierce, and Joan Myers. *Santiago: Saint of Two Worlds.* Albuquerque: University of New Mexico Press, 1991.

Whitefield, Peter. *The Charting of the Oceans: Ten Centuries of Maritime Maps.* Rohnert Park, California: Pomegranate Artbooks, 1996.

Zweig, Stefan. *Conqueror of the Seas: The Story of Magellan.* New York: Viking Press, 1938.

BIBLIOGRAPHY
FOR YOUNG READERS

Blackwood, Alan. *Ferdinand Magellan*. New York: Franklin Watts, Inc., 1986.

Hargrove, Jim. *Ferdinand Magellan*. Chicago: Children's Press, 1990.

Levinson, Nancy Smiler. *Magellan and the First Voyage Around the World*. New York: Clarion Books, 2001.

Mattern, Joanne. *The Travels of Ferdinand Magellan*. New York: Raintree Steck-Vaughn, 2000.

Meltzer, Milton. *Ferdinand Magellan: First to Sail Around the World*. Tarrytown, New York: Benchmark Books, 2001.

Stefoff, Rebecca. *Ferdinand Magellan and the Discovery of the World Ocean*. New York: Chelsea House Publishers, 1990.

Twist, Clint. *Magellan and Da Gama: To the Far East and Beyond*. New York: Raintree Steck-Vaughn, 1994.

Wilkie, Katharine Elliott. *Ferdinand Magellan: Noble Captain*. Boston: Houghton Mifflin College, 2000.

ABOUT THE AUTHOR

Michele Torrey became fascinated with Magellan when she stumbled upon an encyclopedia article about the drama and perils of his circumnavigation of the globe. An explorer herself, she has traveled to almost thirty countries, including Jamaica, the former Czechoslovakia, Belize, China, and Thailand. She now lives with her husband in Washington state, where she was born. This is her sixth book for young readers.